PATRICIA KEYSON

◆

BEYOND THE TOUCH OF TIME

Complete and Unabridged

LINFORD
Leicester

First published in Great Britain in 2017

First Linford Edition
published 2019

A catalogue record for this book is available
from the British Library.

ISBN 978–1–4448–4132–9

Published by
F. A. Thorpe (Publishing)
Anstey, Leicestershire

Set by Words & Graphics Ltd.
Anstey, Leicestershire
Printed and bound in Great Britain by
T. J. International Ltd., Padstow, Cornwall

This book is printed on acid-free paper

BEYOND THE TOUCH OF TIME

A Victorian locket links four stories together, spanning across decades. An aristocrat falls in love with his maid, and heartbreak lies ahead. During World War Two, best friends Barbara and Doreen experience closeness but also jealousy. A young single mother in the 1960s is given the locket, but traumatic events ensue after she casts it aside. And in the present day, Rachel discovers the locket at a car boot sale and wonders about the past of her new talisman, as well as what kind of future it might bring her.

1

RACHEL — Present day

Rachel had only bought two plates and three cups and saucers. Not the most successful of mornings at the car boot sale. It had started to rain and time was flying by. Perhaps she'd be luckier next Sunday. On her way to the car, she stopped. It was virtually impossible for her to ignore a cardboard box on the edge of a table.

'What's in that?' she asked the woman who was trying to protect her goods from the rain, which had intensified.

'I haven't sorted it yet,' the woman replied.

Rachel turned to leave, but her fingers were itching to root through the box to discover what lay hidden inside. 'How much for the whole thing?' she asked.

'You can have it for a tenner.'

Rachel would have paid twenty just for curiosity value, but she prided herself on being a good car booter and loved to haggle. 'Eight?'

'Done,' said the woman.

Rachel hefted the box, hoping the flimsy package wouldn't disintegrate before she reached the car.

Time was not on her side, and the wet weather slowed the traffic towards town. Thank goodness for her other half, Michael, and her auntie, Mo. At nearly thirty, Rachel felt happy and content. She had a remarkable family, her own business, and a man she would be happy to spend the rest of her life with. On top of that, thanks to her maternal grandparents' astute investments, she owned a flat within walking distance of her café in the centre of Cambridge.

Placing the mysterious box on her bed, Rachel changed into her uniform of black trousers and top before pulling on a waterproof and heading to work.

*   *   *

When she arrived at The Corner Café, something didn't seem right. Michael and Mo were nowhere to be seen, and behind the counter there was a red-headed young man who she didn't recognise.

'Can I help you?' asked the lad.

'I hope so,' began Rachel. 'What's your name?'

'I'm Sean.' The Irish accent lilted pleasantly.

'And what are you doing here?' she asked.

'I could be serving you.'

'Where's Mo?'

'Rachel, is that you?' Mo came out from the kitchen, wiping her hands on a towel. 'I need to talk to you.'

Rachel heard her aunt out, but even after giving her mind time to take in what Mo said, she was still unable to react. Served her right for being so cocky and confident about her luck such a short while ago.

Mo handed over a thin white envelope with Rachel's name scrawled on the front. She took it with trembling hands, not wanting to open it. Voices reached her from the front of the café and she knew she'd have to get a grip, open the letter and get on with things.

Tears were not an option for Rachel. She hated the reaction and pity they evoked from onlookers. *Sum up the facts and deal with them later*, she instructed herself. *Michael has left, he's found someone else, he's not coming back to you.*

★   ★   ★

Rachel stuffed the envelope into her trouser pocket and asked, 'Mo, what's Sean doing here?'

'Isn't he lovely?' sighed her aunt. 'Just after Michael left, Sean came in to see if we had any vacancies. What could I do? I didn't promise him anything apart from a trial period of an hour or so and a free meal.'

'He seems okay,' acknowledged Rachel, tying on an apron and washing her hands. 'He doesn't look very old, does he?'

The nasty weather brought people rushing in out of the rain looking for something warming. No one appeared to mind waiting in line, and they were soon chatting among themselves, egged on by Sean. For all his youthful appearance, he had a pleasant way with people.

By four o'clock, the café was almost empty and the stack of rolls and cakes had almost all been sold. The soup kettle was dry and the three of them were tired.

'Go off home, Mo. You've stayed longer than you should have done. I appreciate your help, but go on, shoo.'

'I'm sorry it's been a dreadful day for you,' Mo said.

Rachel shrugged. 'No problem. You've helped an awful lot.' She lowered her voice to a whisper. 'Shall we keep Sean?'

That brought a smile to her aunt's face. 'Yeah, he's cute!'

When Mo had left, Rachel said to

Sean, 'You must be starving. Sit down and have something to eat with me, and some hot coffee.' She pulled open the till and extracted some notes. 'Here, Sean, you've been a great asset today. I don't know how we would have managed without you.'

Sean took the money and stuffed it into his back pocket. 'Thanks. I don't suppose there's any chance of some more shifts, is there?'

'I can't offer you full-time work, but now our other part-time assistant seems to have left, we do have a vacancy.' It took all Rachel's strength of will to keep her voice level as she referred to her beloved Michael as merely a part-time assistant.

'I'm a student,' he said. 'I need the money. I've no work experience apart from having a paper round when I was at school. Does that count, do you think?'

Rachel laughed. 'Yes, I think it could.' She was curious. 'What are you studying?'

'Archaeology. Just starting. Any extra money will be helpful for compulsory field trips, stuff like that. Would you take me on? I can work most mornings and weekends.'

'How about Thursday and Friday mornings and then whatever hours I need you at the weekends?'

She added his contact details into her phone.

★　★　★

Rachel turned on some music and started the cleaning routine, hoping to numb her thoughts. She still couldn't bring herself to think about Michael while there was work to be done. While she cleaned, she reflected on what improvements could be made to the café premises.

Her head was full of plans that went nowhere. At least she'd got through the cleaning and she hadn't thought of Michael.

When she returned home, Rachel wondered how she'd missed the fact that Michael's belongings were not in the flat before she'd left for work. He didn't live there on a permanent basis, preferring to divide his time between her place and a cottage he owned in a nearby village. It had seemed reasonable to her, but now she thought about it, she wondered if the person he'd left her for had been there. Maybe they even lived there with him. Even though she had no audience, she was too well disciplined to break down and cry. Her sisters had sobbed their way through school, their hearts breaking every five minutes. She wasn't like that.

However, thinking of her family, she realised she missed them dreadfully. Rachel's parents and sister, Alice, had moved south to Cornwall a while ago. Her other sister, Lesley, fancied a life of travelling and was now living in Australia. Rachel preferred to stay put. And at least her Aunt Mo was still here.

She poured herself a large glass of wine and sat on the settee staring into space. No one knew what lay ahead, but she had hoped she was in with a chance of a rosy future. Not that her past had been that bad. All in all, she'd been lucky, she supposed. Not many people got to thirty years old with no major trauma in their lives. She put down the glass of wine, knowing she was getting maudlin. There was no way she could, or wanted to, settle in the flat on her own, so she grabbed her coat and went for a walk by the river.

★   ★   ★

'Hi, Rachel.'

She hadn't been expecting to meet anyone she knew. 'Sean? Hi. Where are you off to?'

He shrugged his shoulders and fell into step beside her. 'Nowhere special, just exploring. I'm meeting up with friends later.'

'I came out for fresh air.'

Sean didn't seem in a rush to go anywhere. Rachel felt herself unwinding. 'What made you choose to study archaeology, Sean?'

He became animated, gesturing with his hands, his words quick and enthusiastic. 'When you dig into the past, it's amazing to realise how people's lives influence things even years and years later. I mean, like, I could dig up the remains of someone or something from a barrow or cairn and be able to find out how they existed, what sort of dwelling they had, what they ate, that sort of thing. It's exciting to be able to trace how they've influenced our lives even after a massively long time. And if you find something personal, like a piece of pottery or a ring or bracelet, some sort of jewellery, you learn more about the people and can compare them with us and how we live today. I find the past fascinating.' He paused for breath and ran his fingers through his hair. 'What about you? The café's yours, is it?'

Rachel nodded. 'I love it. It's hard work, but I enjoy it. Things didn't go well today. As you know, a member of staff, someone I thought I knew and trusted, left me in the lurch. No warning, nothing. Just up and went!'

'But you got me instead,' said Sean. Rachel could see his eyes twinkling as the lights from the riverside bars and restaurants illuminated the passers-by. His copper-coloured hair shone and his freckled face broke into a cheeky grin.

'I did,' was all she said.

Sean waved to someone in a pizza parlour and said to Rachel, 'There's one of the people I'm meeting. Would you like to join us?'

Rachel considered the invitation. She didn't want to go home to an empty flat with her desolate thoughts for company, but she wouldn't intrude on Sean's evening. 'Perhaps another time. See you.'

*   *   *

When she got home, Rachel found her phone on the table, where she'd accidentally left it. There was a text

11

from Michael asking her to call him. He could go to hell. As her finger hovered over the button to switch off her phone, the ringtone burst through the silent flat and Michael's smiling face appeared on the tiny screen.

2

'Rachel, please don't hang up. I just want to explain.'

For a while, all she heard was Michael's ragged breath. Then he said, 'What I did was unforgiveable. I should have had the courage to face you and say I was going. I'm sorry.'

Silence hung between them.

'Rachel, are you still there?'

'Yes,' she replied, desperately trying to keep the wobble out of her voice. 'I'm still here, and you're right, what you did was unforgiveable. When I went out this morning, you were in my bed; and when I went into the café expecting to see you there, I was given a note to say you'd taken off with someone else and weren't coming back. What sort of a game was that?'

'I was rude and stupid. I'm sorry.'

Rachel slumped into a chair and

closed her eyes, waiting for a prominent emotion to surface. 'Has anything changed?' she asked eventually. The silence on the line told her all she needed to know.

'I don't like to leave you in the lurch at work. I know it'll be difficult for you and Mo to manage.'

Rachel almost laughed out loud. No mention of their personal relationship, just business. 'We'll be fine, Michael. I won't keep you. Get back to your lover.' She ended the call and turned off the phone. It must have taken some courage to speak to her, Rachel supposed, but Michael had handled the situation very badly. Irritation sandpapered the inside of her, and she couldn't keep still. Suddenly remembering the box of unknown goodies from the car boot sale, she went to retrieve her purchases, hoping to keep her mind off Michael.

It seemed a lifetime ago that she'd splashed through the rain, and she'd all but forgotten the pretty crockery she'd

14

bought. Rachel liked to display the cakes in the café on plates; the cups and saucers, while not being used for drinks, looked attractive dotted around the premises. They were put to one side to be washed thoroughly later.

Now to the box. She carried it into the living area and upended it carefully onto the rug. Kneeling, she picked out items randomly and sorted them into piles. Then she found a small notebook. She made herself more comfortable and opened it. She'd flick through it and then decide what to do with it.

What she read was a shopping list and a collection of recipes — cakes, by the look of it. Forgetting she was supposed to be giving it a cursory going-over, Rachel became engrossed and read the whole thing from beginning to end.

Putting the notebook on the coffee table, she turned her attention to the pile of jewellery, knowing it would have to be sorted at some point. She picked up the largest piece and turned it over in her hand, trying to decide what it was. It was golden in colour with red and blue flashes on the front. She peered at it closely. With a good imagination, it could be a lily of the valley, some sort of flower anyway, depicted on the front. It could have been the pendant of a necklace, but there was no chain. Then she spotted a small hinge on one side. A locket. Gently, she put her nail into the side opposite the hinge and wiggled it. It opened, and Rachel gasped as she looked inside. Two faces appeared, one on either side of the locket: a man and a woman. Obviously a love token. They both looked young, and she found herself wondering what had happened to them. Why had the locket been discarded? Was there a tragic tale behind this piece of jewellery? More likely, it was just inherited stuff which wasn't wanted. She couldn't bear the thought of these two people being discarded again, so she fetched a pin and levered out the pictures. Behind the drawings was yet another layer of a past Rachel knew nothing about: a curl of hair.

At first glance, Rachel had thought the locket was ugly, but now she changed her mind completely. Nothing containing such items could be called that. The locket and its contents were placed on the coffee table with the notebook. She yawned widely; it was definitely time for bed.

*   *   *

Rachel had slept deeply and was woken by the alarm. Monday morning and just her and Aunt Mo. The November morning was chilly, and a hot coffee would be welcome. She was the first to arrive and set to work getting things out of the fridge and arranging them on the counter and display unit. Tom from the bakery would be along soon with the daily bread order.

Mo beat him to it. 'Hi, Rachel.' She brought a cold gust of air in the door with her. 'Sleep okay?'

'Yeah, I did. I had a good evening, in fact.' She was about to tell her aunt about the things from the car boot sale when the phone rang. 'The Corner Café,' she said. She listened and then exploded, 'What? I can't believe this. No, it's not your fault. It's good of you to check with me. It'll be too late for today, but I'll send over the order for the rest of the week ASAP. Thanks.'

She put the phone down and turned to Mo, shaking her head. 'Michael forgot to put through the bread order for this week. That was the bakery asking if it was a mistake. Tom's already on his rounds and won't be able to get anything to us before this afternoon. We'll have to make our own arrangements.' Rachel thought quickly and dashed to open the freezer. 'Here, defrost these.' She handed over some packets. 'I'm off to the supermarket.'

A short while later, Rachel barrelled through the door of The Corner Café with her arms full, and found herself face to face with a handsome stranger who tried to help her with her purchases.

'It's fine,' she panted. 'Thank you, but I can manage.' She darted behind the counter, then looked back at the man. He was tall and wearing a dark suit. 'We had a bit of a hiccup with the bread delivery this morning,' she explained. They exchanged smiles, but Rachel was aware the man was preparing to leave.

'Thank you. See you again, I hope,' she said.

'I enjoyed the bacon and cheese scone, and I've warmed up, so thank you. And, yes, I'm sure I'll be popping in again soon. I'm Roy.'

Rachel was conscious of Mo's look, but she chose to ignore it. She was still smarting from the break-up with Michael. The only thing that had got her through last night was the thrill of unpacking the box from the car boot sale. As she toasted and filled bagels, her mind kept returning to the notebook and the locket with its hidden contents.

At last there was a lull in the queue of customers, and Mo said, 'Coffee?'

'Please,' replied Rachel. 'While there's a bit of respite, I'll get the week's order in to the bakery.'

'Don't forget the mince pies.'

'What? You're joking, right?' Rachel was amazed. 'It's only November,' she reminded Mo.

'And soon it'll be December.'

Rachel knew her aunt very well. 'Are you making me do all this to take my mind off Michael? Did you sabotage the bakery order to have me running around the town looking for bread? I wouldn't put it past you. Did you plant Roy as a diversion?' She narrowed her eyes and tried to hide her grin. 'He's much too old for me.'

Quick as a flash, Mo came back with, 'I'll have him, then!'

★   ★   ★

The next few days passed busily but uneventfully. On Thursday, Rachel was pleased to see Sean, having drafted him in for a few hours over the next few days.

A flurry of customers arrived. Rachel heard, 'A bacon and cheese scone, please.'

'Sorry,' said Sean, 'I don't think we do scones, but I'll check. They sound tasty, don't they?' He looked towards Rachel.

She felt her face flaring as she recognised Roy. 'They were just a one-off,' she said.

'Pity,' said Roy. Replying to Sean, he added, 'They were delicious. Okay then, I'll have some leek and kale soup, please, with granary bread.'

'Good choice,' said Sean with a smile, taking his money.

When the soup was ready, Rachel took it to Roy's table. Why she'd told Mo he was too old, she had no idea. He looked serious, and his dark hair was greying above his ears, but he was probably only a little older than she was.

When there was a slight lull, Sean asked if he could have a quick break, as he had to run a few errands.

Mo turned to Rachel and said, 'Are you all right? I'm really sorry about you and Michael, but I don't know how to help you. I do feel for you, though. Believe me, I can remember what it feels like to have a broken heart.' She placed her hand gently on Rachel's arm. 'I know you're not heavy on outward shows of emotions, but please remember that I love you dearly.'

Not trusting herself to speak, Rachel just nodded.

Sean returned, banging the café door behind him. 'I see next door's up for sale. Let's hope it's not going to open up as a coffee shop!'

3

Rachel wondered why her neighbours were selling up. Years ago, their shop had been a thriving general store with a post office. They sold anything and everything, but Rachel hardly went in there now as she scurried past it between work and her home.

'I'm just popping next door,' she said to Mo, putting one lemon and one raspberry muffin in a bag.

She opened the door to the shop and looked around. It was in a dreadful condition. An old woman with straggly white hair, wearing a dirty coat, was hovering beside almost-empty shelves.

'Flo, is that you? It's Rachel from the café next door. I've brought you and Stan some cake.' She held out the bag.

Flo grabbed it and almost tore it open. 'Just what I want,' she said. 'Stan's not well; he's had a couple of falls and now they say he's had a stroke. He's in the hospital.'

Rachel put out her hand to the old woman. 'I'm really sorry. Is there any way I can help make things better?'

Flo shook her head. 'Things aren't going to get better. We're up for sale, as you can see. I'm shutting up the shop today and moving into Heathfield House at the end of next week. Stan will join me when, and if, he's allowed out of the hospital.' She looked around the shop, her eyes bright. 'We had some good times here. A lot has happened and now we're at the end of the road. Bit sad, isn't it?'

Rachel thought it was the most heart-rending thing she'd been witness to. She cleared her throat before trusting herself to speak. 'Will someone be able to oversee the sale for you?'

A smile lit Flo's face. 'Yes, the estate agent is wonderful. He said he'll see to everything; even offered to come by and help me with clearing stock and things if I want him to.'

'There are some good people around, aren't there?'

⋆   ⋆   ⋆

Later, after closing the café, Rachel cleaned as usual and then found she was in no hurry to return home. She decided she'd make some scones, not just because Roy had found them delicious, but also because it would be something she enjoyed doing. As she methodically measured, weighed and mixed, she found herself contemplating the issue she hadn't yet faced up to: Michael. Michael had let her down, and she was surprised to realise that her pride had been more broken than her heart. There was no yearning for him to come back, and she wondered if she hadn't been in love with him after all.

Two batches of scones were cooling on racks in the limited kitchen area of the café when Rachel heard a noise overhead. It was no doubt Flo sorting out some of her things. There was certainly a lot of banging about, and Rachel thought that she would go and ask if things were okay.

A knock on her door alarmed her. She looked out of the window, and in the gloom of the evening, she saw it was Roy.

'We're closed, but come on in, it's freezing out there.'

'Something smells good.' He shut the door behind him. 'Scones. You knew I was coming, then!'

Rachel laughed. 'Seems I did. Actually, I'm a bit concerned. My neighbour's elderly and there's been some banging going on next door. I'm not sure whether or not to interfere. What do you think?'

'Flo Baxter, you mean? It's okay, I've just left her. She's moving and I'm helping with some of the heavier things.'

'Oh, it was *you*. You're the kind estate agent? I must say, you don't look it.'

Roy put his head to one side and grinned at her. 'Flatterer!'

'Oh, I didn't mean . . . I didn't take you for an estate agent. Would you like a scone to make up for my mouth being engaged without my brain's knowledge?'

'What about dinner? I'm starving.'

'Now that's a good idea. So am I!'

★   ★   ★

The Chinese restaurant was tucked away close to the theatre, a short walk from the café. It was crowded, but Roy was greeted like a regular and they were shown to a table near the window.

Roy glanced at her. 'What shall we order?'

'You choose,' she said. 'I'm happy to try whatever you recommend.'

'Shall we get some food to share?'

'Great, sounds just right. Can I have a beer, please?'

Roy ordered it and tea for himself. 'I have to drive home later. Perhaps you also have to. Tell me about yourself.'

'For a start, I live within a very short walk of the café, so no, I'm not driving home. As to telling you about myself,

27

I'd like you to tell me *your* story first. How did you end up being an estate agent?'

'Well, I had an uneventful upbringing, left school with fairly good results and then had no idea what to do next. An estate agent friend of the family asked me to show some people over a property as they were short-staffed, and I was hooked. Now, your turn.'

'I had a most unconventional upbringing,' said Rachel. 'My parents were mad. Still are! Anyway, I always enjoyed cooking, and opening the café has been the best thing I've ever done.'

The next couple of hours passed quickly, and soon it was time to leave.

'It's been fun,' Rachel said.

'I'll walk you home.' Roy helped her into her coat and held the door open as they braved the chilly night air.

'It's fine,' replied Rachel. 'I'm capable of getting myself home without mishap.'

Roy continued walking along with her, and she enjoyed his company.

'This is me,' said Rachel, stopping

outside her apartment block. 'Thanks again, and I hope I'll see you soon.'

Inside her flat, Rachel acknowledged that she felt happy. After she'd showered and got into her cosy pyjamas, she looked at herself in the mirror. A slim woman of average height, jet black hair cut in a neat chin-length bob, and radiant grey eyes. Nothing like the tragic figure she'd thought herself to be just a few days ago.

*   *   *

On Sunday morning, Rachel awoke with a thumping headache. She'd intended to go to the airfield car boot sale again, but as she had to be at work later, her priority was to get herself feeling better. Fresh air could be the answer, so she made tea and then pulled on a pair of ancient jogging bottoms, a T-shirt and fleece, and a thick anorak. The temperature had crashed and it was freezing cold outside. Frost rimed the hedges and frozen cobwebs glistened, giving a magical appearance to the morning. She inhaled the clean-smelling air, feeling a little better already.

Her phone rang. She looked at the incoming number. 'Hi, Mum.'

'Christmas!' came the reply.

'Erm, okay. How are you?'

'We're fine, darling. Now I've got to tell you that Dad has been doing some research down here, trying to find out what our next project will be.'

Rachel had heard it all before. Her parents wanted to live lives without boring routines, just exhilaration, pleasure and something to fuel them with excitement.

'I suppose he's researched Cornish pasties, Rick Stein's fish restaurant and how many escaped convicts there are roaming about on Bodmin Moor,' she teased.

'All good ideas, thanks, Rachel. Anyway, I'm calling to save you from feeling you have to rush down here and be a dutiful daughter by visiting your family at Christmas. We won't be here.

Dad and I have booked a retreat for the whole Christmas period. And Alice is volunteering at a Christmas charity refuge shelter. I'll let Mo know. You stay and have a nice time with Michael.'

She started to explain that Michael was no longer around, but her mother had ended the call. Rachel half-admired and half-despaired of her parents' hippy style of living. But she was pleased they seemed fulfilled and happy.

By the time Rachel arrived at work, her headache had cleared. Sean and Mo were both at the café before her and she brought them up to date with her family's news. Mo didn't say much, but Rachel had noticed she'd been a bit preoccupied over the last few days.

'Cool parents,' said Sean.

'Do you have a large family, Sean?' asked Rachel.

'I'm Irish,' he said. 'Of course I do. There's Mum and Dad, my sisters, Ciara, Aoife . . . ' He counted them off on his fingers.

'Okay, I get the picture,' laughed Rachel.

'What are you doing for Christmas?'

'I should go home, but I don't want to let you down. You gave me a job here and I don't want to mess things up and get the sack.'

'That's okay, you should be with your family,' she replied.

★   ★   ★

It proved to be a surprisingly busy Sunday morning and around half past two, the three of them took advantage of a lull.

'I've been thinking,' sighed Rachel. 'It would be nice if I could cook some hot meals.'

'Well then, why don't you?' asked Sean, biting into a cheese and mushroom toasted bagel.

'No room,' replied Rachel. 'The kitchen simply isn't big enough, just look.'

'Those scones you made were great,' continued Sean. 'You should make those more often. Sorry if I'm speaking out of turn.'

Rachel shook her head. 'It's good to know what people think. Roy liked them as well. What do you think, Mo?' There was no answer, and when Rachel looked at her aunt, she saw there was a faraway look in her eye and she doubted she'd been following the conversation at all. 'Okay, you two. You can go home if you like.'

Sean said he'd go, and there was no reply yet again from Mo. When they were on their own, Rachel said, 'Mo, what's up? You're quiet, and that's unusual for you. Tell me.'

'I've got a few things on my mind at the moment, Rachel. Sorry, I can't tell you, not just yet, but I will soon. Nothing's wrong, I'm not ill or anything like that. See you tomorrow.'

★   ★   ★

Rachel had a peculiar feeling when she opened the front door of her flat. Usually on a Sunday, she and Michael went home together. She gathered up

33

the dirty washing, which she loaded into the machine. She decided that she would have a clear-out, make sure all of Michael's belongings and all reminders of him were eradicated, and have things how *she* wanted them. She put on some music and bounced around, organising her belongings. Her thoughts turned to Roy. He was a lovely man, he was easy company, he made her laugh, he was polite and considerate — oh, and he was also attractive. She laughed at her thoughts, happy that the flat felt hers again.

After a hot shower, she pulled on her pyjamas and went into the sitting room thinking she'd see what was on the television. Then she saw the notebook and locket on the coffee table where she'd left them a week ago. The television was instantly forgotten, and Rachel settled happily on the settee with her feet tucked under her and her head resting on a soft cushion as she examined her treasures again.

4

Over the next days, Rachel's life tilted further.

She was just about to shut the café when Sean pushed open the door. 'Hi,' she said. 'What are you doing here?'

He ran his fingers through his tousled hair. 'Rachel, I'm really sorry. I couldn't let you know earlier, as I've only just found out myself. I'll no longer be available for work during the day. I'm letting you down big time.'

'You have to do what's best for you, Sean. It's been great having you around, and you're a big hit with the customers.'

'I'll have to get another job after Christmas. It'll need to be in the evenings.' He smiled. 'I warn you, though, this isn't the last time you'll see me.' He held out his hand to her. 'Merry Christmas, in case I don't see you again before the holidays.'

Rachel ignored the outstretched hand and pulled him into a cuddle. 'You too. By the way, I think The Tiffin Carrier is looking for delivery people for the new year. I'll give you a good reference.'

'Thanks,' said Sean as he left.

Pulling out her phone, she speed-dialled and was soon connected with Mo. She told her about Sean, then added, 'We'll manage, won't we? On our own?'

'Of course we will,' came the reply. 'Rachel, will you come and eat with me tonight at The Juicy Date down the road?'

'It's that new Moroccan restaurant, isn't it? Sounds great. Half seven?'

As soon as she'd ended the call, Rachel realised she couldn't put off getting on to the agency about someone to help out over the Christmas period. She would need someone for longer now that Sean wasn't coming back.

★ ★ ★

'This is amazing,' declared Rachel, looking at the lamb tagine she'd ordered. 'I'd love to be able to serve things like this in the café.' She put her head to one side and considered. 'I think I'd add more cinnamon.'

Mo laughed. 'Rachel, you're a born gourmet. And I think it's time for you to expand your wings.'

'In what way?' Rachel was puzzled.

'Have a place where you can open in the evenings, and have room to cook what you'd like to, what you'd enjoy making. You've too many talents to hide them away.'

'You know it's not possible. There's just no room.'

'There could be, though.' Mo took a sip of wine. 'I hope you won't be cross . . . I'm considering putting in an offer on Flo and Stan's place.'

'Really? What will you use it for?'

'I'll give it to you!' Without waiting for a reply, she plunged on. 'There's the same amount of money left for Alice and Lesley, so I've been scrupulously fair.'

A choke escaped Rachel. 'Auntie, dearest, are you out of your mind?'

'Possibly. But I'm serious, Rachel. I love you dearly. You're like a daughter to me and I think the world of you. Let me do this for you. Please.'

Rachel couldn't think of anything to say. It was what she wanted. But it was impossible. Wasn't it?

'Let's enjoy the rest of our meal, and then will you come home with me and discuss things?'

They left the restaurant and shivered their way to Mo's house a short walk away.

Lounging in a comfortable armchair by her aunt's fire, Rachel said, 'Mo, tell me what you've done. What's it all about?'

'I told you. I want you to have the premises next door to the café and make your dream come true. It's achievable, Rachel. As I said, I want to put in an offer, and I'm sure it will be accepted, especially as I'm a cash buyer.'

A thought occurred to Rachel. 'Is Roy in on this with you? Is it a conspiracy?'

'No.' Mo sounded shocked. 'Of course not. I didn't deal with Roy, it was someone called Nancy.'

Rachel shook her head. 'I can't let you do this, Mo.' As her aunt opened her mouth to speak, Rachel held up her hand. 'If, and I mean *if*, I let you go ahead on my behalf, I won't let you pay for all of it.'

'You're warming to it, then?' Mo's eyes sparkled.

Rachel yawned and nodded, her eyes drooping. She hauled herself up and threw her arms around her aunt. 'I love you, Mo. Thank you. I don't just mean for the café proposition, I mean for everything.'

5

Scarlett arrived late to her first morning shift at The Corner Café. Rachel greeted her politely, showed her around the tiny café and described her duties. All she had to do was take orders and money.

'Yeah, looks dead simple,' said Scarlett, placing herself behind the counter and getting out her phone.

Rachel raised her eyebrows at Mo, but said nothing.

After half an hour of inaccurate orders and complaints of wrong change, Rachel said, 'I know it's all new to you, Scarlett, but please try to get things right. It's important that the customers are happy.'

'Yeah, okay,' came a rather sullen reply.

'And please may I ask that you leave your phone in your pocket until your break.'

'I'm expecting some serious phone

calls, I can't just ignore them.'

'Yes, you can, at least while you're working,' Rachel insisted.

Things improved slightly, but Rachel knew Scarlett's attitude was not what she wanted from an employee in her café. She called the agency but they told her there was no one else available.

'Mo, what am I to do? Scarlett isn't what we want, is she? But if there's no alternative, what should we do?'

'Ditch her,' said Mo, not taking her eyes from the panini press.

Rachel sighed. 'I'll give her one more chance tomorrow.' Then her attention was taken by a customer joining the short queue. Roy. They made eye contact and smiled at each other.

Rachel continued with the orders she'd received, anxious to get them to the customers with minimal delay. When Roy's was ready, she took it to him. 'Nice to see you again, Roy. Here's your wrap.'

'Er, sorry, Rachel, it's not what I ordered. I'm not too fond of eggs. I asked for a tuna and mayo bap.'

'Sorry, new member of staff,' she whispered. 'I'll get you a tuna mayo and it's on the house.'

When she returned, she asked, 'Have you plans for Christmas?' Why she was making small talk with him when they were busy, Rachel had no idea, but she wanted to keep chatting with him.

He smiled at her. 'Visiting my family, seeing friends, usual sort of thing. What about you?'

'I'm only taking Christmas Day off.'

'Sounds as if you work too hard.' He frowned at her. 'I learnt ages ago there's more to life than the daily grind.' Taking a sip of coffee, he added, 'I hope we'll be able to meet up soon.'

'That's something to look forward to,' replied Rachel.

★   ★   ★

The agency phoned the following morning to inform Rachel that Scarlett had fallen over and broken her arm, and was therefore unable to work. Rachel asked if she'd get a replacement. Unfortunately, there was still no one available.

'It doesn't matter,' stated Mo. 'We'll manage.'

Rachel shook her head. 'No, we won't. We won't be able to give our customers the best service. We're stretched. We'll have to close for a bit.'

'Now that,' said Mo, 'is the most sensible thing you've said for a while. You haven't had a break, not even a day off, since you opened. Except Christmas Day.'

'You're right,' acknowledged Rachel, wondering if she might spend some time with Roy. She'd like to get to know him better. 'What I'd like to do, with your agreement, is stay open until the new year and then have some time off. Sound okay to you?'

Her aunt said, 'If the sale goes through as I hope it will, then there'll be renovations to be done, and there's obviously no way you can stay open then. You'll probably have to close for about three months.'

'What!' exploded Rachel. 'Three months! I was thinking something like three days.'

Mo shook her head. 'Think about it. It has to be done, Rachel. If you want a proper restaurant, then the building work will have to be done properly.'

Rachel conceded the point. 'I hadn't thought it through. I'd just seen the end product, but you're right, of course. It's still a frightening prospect, though.' She was surprised to find her throat constricting and knew tears were threatening, but, as usual, she wouldn't let them flow.

'You're exhausted, Rachel. You need a break. Now, I've got one or two things to do, so if it's okay with you, I'll buzz off, but I'll be back before you leave.'

When Mo returned, she looked happy and bouncy. 'I'm helping with the cleaning this afternoon — no buts. And while we get on with it, I'll outline my plan. Tell me what you think.'

'How many other tricks have you got up those baggy sleeves of yours?' asked Rachel.

'A company looking for host families for international students got in touch with me through the U3A — the volunteer-led group I'm a member of. They've a woman who's quite a bit older than the rest of her group and they asked if I could take her over Christmas. The woman, Renata, is Spanish and is keen to learn as much English as she can, and mix with as many different people as possible. I'm sure Renata will be happy to come and help out here for the Christmas period.'

Rachel narrowed her eyes. 'You haven't met her, have you? What if she's awful?'

'I'll give her the once-over and then decide. If you trust me, that is,' she sniffed.

Rachel laughed. 'I hope she's okay. You're the one saddled with her over Christmas whether she is or not.'

★ ★ ★

Rachel needn't have worried. Renata was around Mo's age, and was curvaceous and lively as well as colourful. Her long, curly black hair was caught back with a bright tangerine scarf. She wove a Mediterranean atmosphere around the café as Mo proudly ushered her in, and the three of them bonded immediately.

'What a wonderful café.' Renata grabbed Rachel's arm and squeezed it. She peered into her face. 'You look like your aunt. I want to thank you for your help in giving me a good time in England. The other people in the group are young and wild. Me, I am old and wild!' As she laughed, her head shook, her large hooped earrings swaying mesmerically.

'Something you have in common with my Aunt Mo,' Rachel said with a nod.

'Tell me what you wish me to do, Rachel. And tell me off when I get distracted.'

Rachel was outlining how the café was run when she was interrupted by Mo.

'I ordered mince pies, lots of mince pies. I took an executive decision and decided you'd like to get into the Christmas spirit and give out free mince pies with every hot drink purchased. I'm paying for them, of course.'

'Bah, humbug,' said Rachel, sighing dramatically, then grinning at her aunt. 'Good idea, but I can't say I'm in the Christmas spirit yet.'

'Better have a mince pie then,' said Renata.

'They're nicer if they're warm.' Mo popped three into the microwave.

Renata took a bite. 'Nice. I had better distance myself from them. I shall be charged excess baggage on the journey home.'

Customers streamed in and were delighted with their freebies. With the scent of spice in the air, there was definitely a festive mood beginning.

'Renata's fun,' whispered Rachel to

Mo as they processed the orders. 'And nice, too.'

Mo nodded. 'Glad you like her, as you'll be spending Christmas with her.'

Rachel's head jerked up. 'What do you mean?'

'Well, you're coming to me for your Christmas meal, aren't you? And I suppose you'll insist the three of us totter into work on Boxing Day.'

Although Rachel knew her aunt was teasing, it got her thinking. Perhaps she'd been taking advantage of Mo without realising it.

★　★　★

Rachel couldn't settle. After taking a hot shower and pulling on jeans and a thick sweater, she picked up the locket and turned it over in her hands. Why was she so drawn to it? She wasn't one for over-sentimentality, but she felt a connection.

She prised it open and looked at the emptiness. Something was wrong. In a flash, she knew what needed to be done. The contents of the locket had to be replaced. When she'd done that, the locket was stuffed into her fleece pocket and she stepped out into the cold evening air, wanting to think through the plans which had been mooted for the renovation of her café. She stood opposite the premises and tried to look at it dispassionately. The exterior was badly in need of decorating, some of the paint was peeling, and the shop next door was in an even worse condition, making the whole corner area completely lacking in any kerb appeal. Whatever the internal layout of the shop, it could be altered to suit her. She would definitely need to have a proper look around the inside.

Rachel was about to return home when a ghost walk guide leading a group made her smile. He was one of the more inventive ones, and she was intrigued as to what he would come up with. He stopped and gestured dramatically with his multi-coloured umbrella.

'That pub over there, The Dragonfly, is one of the town's most ancient watering holes. I myself have been witness to ghostly activities in the snug bar. We shouldn't be distracted by the superficial name, Dragonfly. A dragonfly is more than a transitory insect. Its ephemeral nature should not be underestimated. The blink of an eye, a baby's breath, transcends the touch of time.'

Rachel's head and neck prickled as goosebumps broke out over her skin. Instinctively, her hand covered the locket in her zipped-up pocket.

6

Rachel slept soundly that night. She was awake early, feeling refreshed. Her hand reached out to touch the locket by her bedside, as if it were a lucky charm. Then her attention turned to Flo. How was she getting on? Was she on her own, or had Stan been allowed home to join her?

There was plenty of time before she needed to get to work, so Rachel showered and, with a bathrobe around her, took flour, sugar and eggs out of the cupboard. She'd bake some cakes and take them to Heathfield House.

In her imagination, she saw a lovely big kitchen on the new premises. She knew it would be very expensive, and there was no way she'd let Mo pay for everything. She reached for her phone. 'Mo, I really can't let you pay for the new premises,' said Rachel.

'Okay, it's your choice.' The call was ended.

Rachel felt sick. Not because she might have cut off her nose to spite her face, but because she was worried she'd upset Mo.

She picked up the phone again. 'Mo, what I should have said was that I can't let you pay for *all* of it. I would like to have some sort of financial input. The only way I can do that is if I sell my flat.'

'We'll talk about it later, shall we? Renata's just cooked me the most enormous Spanish omelette and I can't be rude, can I?'

Rachel laughed. 'Enjoy it!'

★　★　★

Rachel was glad to get things organised before Mo and Renata arrived.

'*Buenos dias*, Rachel,' beamed Renata, hugging her. 'Here, I have brought you some tortilla. You are much too thin, despite all the nice things to eat that you sell in your special café.'

While they worked, Mo said, 'I don't want to take over completely, Rachel, but have you thought about the implications of selling your flat?'

Rachel sighed. 'Probably not, but Mo, I want to have the best I can and it's going to cost loads. I don't know exactly what I have in mind for the new premises, but I think I should start with an inspection of the property. Do you agree?'

Mo nodded. 'Definitely. Shall we make an appointment to view? When shall we go?'

'As soon as possible.'

When it was time for Mo and Renata to leave, they insisted on staying and doing the cleaning. 'Really, it will help with my understanding of the work ethic,' said Renata, her bangles and earrings tinkling as she laughed. 'I have to embrace every bit of England that I can while I am here.'

'I see your English language is perfect,' said Rachel. 'Exactly why are you here?'

'I've been found out, I think. I have lots of friends and interests in Spain, but I want to embrace new things, understand how the world goes round. Do you know what I mean?'

'Yes,' replied Rachel. 'I think I do.'

★   ★   ★

Back at home, after taking the cakes to Heathfield House, Rachel picked up the locket and held it to her neck, wondering what the original chain had looked like and what had happened to it. She threaded it onto a piece of Christmas ribbon and hung it around her neck. Things had changed since she'd come into possession of the locket. Was it fate or coincidence? The notebook with the recipes was a fortuitous find as well, and had been instrumental to her baking that morning. Old-fashioned cakes would certainly be a good line to try in her new venture. She desperately wanted things to work out well. Her fingers clattered over the laptop keys as she made a list of things she desired for her business future. Her personal future would have to take second place — for now at least.

★   ★   ★

Reluctantly, Rachel removed the locket from around her neck before going to work. Her standards of hygiene prevented her from wearing either nail polish or jewellery. She'd have to say something to Renata about her jewellery and she hoped she wouldn't be offended.

'I am quiet this morning,' observed Renata, shaking her head and arms around. 'See, no jewellery. I shall probably make up for it with laughter. I am very happy to be here.'

Rachel couldn't have been more delighted or surprised when Roy visited the shop around mid-morning. Renata made sure he had time to make a selection from the menu, pointed out the flavour of the soup that day and remained smiley and attentive while taking his order.

'Please take a seat and one of us will bring it to you,' Renata said. 'Are you a regular customer? If not, you should be. This is a wonderful café.'

'I agree.' Roy smiled, looking at Rachel.

When she took the food to his table, Rachel perched on the seat next to him. 'I visited Mr and Mrs Baxter, you know; Flo and Stan from next door. He's out of hospital and they seem to be settled happily at Heathfield House.'

'That's good news.'

Rachel nodded her agreement, then hesitated. 'Er, I . . . that is, we . . . are thinking of making an offer on the property. I'd like to have a proper restaurant with better facilities.'

Secretly, she wanted his approval and was astonished when he said, 'So much for cutting down on the hard graft.' She couldn't think of anything to say in reply, so she got up and inched away, disappointed at the coldness of his tone.

Back behind the counter, Mo said, 'By the way, Rachel, I rang Nancy earlier and we've an appointment to view next door when you've finished here today.'

Rachel perked up a bit. 'Brilliant. Thanks, Mo. Will you come with us, Renata?'

'I'd love to, but I'm meeting some of my friends from the group later.'

Renata's comment got Rachel thinking. It had been a while since she'd seen Liz, Gillian and Claire. They used to meet on a regular basis, but things had slowed down since Rachel had met Michael and had started spending most of her time either with him or at the café. She decided she'd send each of them Christmas wishes from her phone.

★   ★   ★

Rachel was waiting outside the café when Mo and Nancy turned up. Mo had a lot of interests and was always off on some errand. Rachel often wondered why she continued to work at the café. She hoped it wasn't out of loyalty or some sort of sympathy for Rachel.

Mo and Nancy were chatting as if they were old friends. 'This is my niece, Rachel Miller, the owner of The Corner Café,' explained Mo.

'And you're wanting to extend your business, is that right?' asked Nancy as she searched for the correct keys to let them into the shop.

Rachel nodded.

It was too dark to see out of the windows, but Nancy filled them in. 'You know there's a small garden at the rear. Needs to be tidied up, but a nice space.'

'The garden, of course.' Rachel was excited. 'I'd forgotten about that. It would be perfect for customers to spill out onto in the summer. And I can grow herbs and make it cheery and colourful with pots of plants.'

When Nancy left them to discuss things in private, Rachel said to Mo,

'What do you think? Do you like it?'

'I don't have to. It'll be your property. Do *you* like it?'

Rachel shook her head. 'No, I don't.' Then she hugged Mo. 'I absolutely *love* it.'

'Keep your voice down or Nancy will expect a higher offer.'

They said goodbye to Nancy and told her they'd be in touch.

'This is all great, Mo,' said Rachel, 'but it still comes down to money. As I said, I shall sell my flat to pay for things like furnishings, staff salaries, that sort of thing.'

'Where will you live, then?'

'I'll rent somewhere.'

'And where will you get the money to pay for that as well as keep a healthy bank balance from the sale of your flat?'

'Mo, you're asking all the wrong questions,' moaned Rachel, knowing she'd backed herself into a corner.

'No, they're the right questions. You just haven't got the right answers yet. But you will. Let me run this idea by you. You rent out your flat, come and live with me and save the money. It'll be wonderful to have your company, Rachel. I promise we won't be on top of each other. Go and think about it.' She kissed her niece and gave her a little push towards home.

When Rachel got indoors, she had a shower, made an omelette and a hot chocolate drink, then sat at her laptop with the notebook in front of her. She reached out for the locket and strung it around her neck. Her plans flowed into the computer as if by magic.

7

A text message alert showed on Rachel's phone. It was Liz answering her tentative enquiry as to what she had been doing since they'd last met. Rachel quickly called her friend's number and soon the two of them were chatting as if there had been no separation.

'I'm going to spend a week with Mum and Dad,' said Liz. 'I expect you'll be spending your time with Michael. Or are you going to Cornwall? And Mo, how's she?'

The conversation flitted from one topic to another. When Rachel explained about Michael, she could hear Liz's sigh down the phone. 'Is that a sigh of exasperation at his behaviour or relief that we've finished?' asked Rachel.

'If I'm honest, a bit of both. But I won't go down either of those roads.'

'Can we meet up in the new year?

I've really missed you and the others.'

'Of course! I'll give you a ring after Christmas. Thanks very much for getting in touch.'

★ ★ ★

It was the evening of Christmas Eve and Rachel was all glammed up. She'd packed a small bag with some clothes for the two nights' stay at Mo's house, along with the gifts she had for her and Renata. She'd been told that Renata was preparing a typical Spanish Christmas meal, which was to be served that evening. Before she left her flat, she sent a text to Roy wishing him an enjoyable Christmas. Then she was ready to go.

Mo came out to greet her niece as she drove her car into the driveway. 'Renata's shooed me out of the kitchen.' She grinned. 'Can't say I'm sorry. Come on in and have a drink. I'm looking forward to having a nice, normal conversation with you away from customers and away from filling rolls and making coffee.'

As soon as the front door opened, Rachel inhaled the most wonderful aroma. 'What is that? What's she making?'

'Whatever it is, it's a huge meal. She ordered loads of things online. Isn't it nice to be waited on?'

'Heavenly,' replied Rachel, sinking into a cosy armchair in Mo's sitting room and closing her eyes. 'I'll take my things up in a moment, is that okay?'

'Of course, but while you're relaxing, I'll talk you through what I think might work if you came to live here in the new year. As you know, I've an en-suite bedroom and along the landing from there is another bedroom which is Renata's at the moment, and a bathroom, which could be yours. We'd have to share the kitchen, but I don't think that would be a problem; we're used to that, aren't we?'

Rachel nodded, her eyes still closed.

'Good. We've made the offer, so we'll

just have to wait until after Christmas to see if Nancy has been able to secure a deal for us. I'm going to have a sherry, as I got some Oloroso in for Renata. Will you try some?'

Rachel shook her head. 'I'll have something lighter, please. Have you any lager?'

Mo went off and returned with a glass of lager and poured a generous measure of sherry into a schooner for herself. 'That's a pretty locket, Rachel. I don't think I've seen it before.' She reached out and touched it gently.

Rachel told her aunt the story of the box of treasures from the car boot sale and was just about to show her the contents of the locket when they heard the kitchen door bang open and Renata calling to them.

'You could smell the alcohol, Renata,' teased Mo. 'Come and have a drink with us.'

Renata's face was red and sweat lightly beaded her forehead, but she was all smiles and good humour as usual.

'Perfect. I hope you're hungry. There's enough for the five thousand out there.'

'It smells delicious,' said Rachel, sitting up and making a toast. 'To a happy Christmas.' She took a sip of her drink. 'I'm being nosy, Renata, but is there a Señor Renata waiting for you at home?'

She chuckled and shook her head. 'There used to be; in fact, there have been three Señor Renatas as you put it. The first one died, the second went off with someone else, and the third one died as well. Not, I might add, after eating my Christmas dinner, though!'

'Oh, I'm sorry,' said Rachel. 'How thoughtless of me.'

Renata hugged her. 'You didn't know. What's past is past.' Her eyes sparkled. 'Who's to say there isn't going to be a fourth Señor Renata coming along soon?'

'And you believe you can find happiness with more than one man? We don't just have one intended person in the world for each of us?'

Renata's eyes widened as she replied, 'Of course not. Let me tell you — my name, Renata, means reborn. So of course I believe that people can be reincarnated from a previous life. As the rebirth of a soul in a new body. Do you find that interesting?'

Rachel found it astounding, and clasped her fingers over the locket around her neck.

★　★　★

'I feel as stuffed as that turkey was,' said Mo, leaning back in her dining chair and patting her stomach.

'We'll walk it off later,' laughed Renata, helping herself to another couple of potatoes and quickly devouring them. 'Did you enjoy it, Rachel?'

'It was delicious.'

When they'd spent a leisurely time sipping coffee and nibbling at assorted cookies, Renata said, 'Time to go, I think.'

Rachel and Mo exchanged a look,

wondering what was in store for them.

The night air was cold with a touch of frost forming. Stars twinkled down on them from a clear sky, and Rachel enjoyed the crispness around them. She knew where they were going: church.

Inside the ancient building, the organ piped out carol music and a choir sang. Anticipation filled the space as people greeted one another and she found herself being embraced by strangers. When she realised they were speaking Spanish, she understood they were friends of Renata.

After the service, they walked home, with members of the group breaking off every now and then as they reached the roads of their respective host families. Rachel and Mo returned the much-repeated *Feliz Navidad* — happy Christmas! And then there were just the three of them.

'Rachel? Is that you?'

She turned and, to her delight, there was Roy, beaming at her. 'Were you at the service? It's a family tradition. See, we're all here.' He gestured towards the people he was with.

What a wonderful coincidence. And Roy showed no sign of animosity; she must have imagined his rather stern tone in the café. 'Renata made us all the most delicious Christmas meal. And then she brought us here.'

'So are you having sandwiches and cold cuts tomorrow?' asked Roy.

'I have a surprise for them,' said Renata with a wink, her face wreathed in a smile. 'Rachel will tell you all about it when you call at the café on Boxing Day.'

★ ★ ★

When Rachel awoke on Christmas morning, it took her a few minutes to remember what day it was and where she was. Sighing deeply and closing her eyes again, she promised herself just a few more minutes' lie-in.

When she surfaced again, it was gone eleven. The sleep had done her good and she was ready for the day ahead.

'Merry Christmas, Rachel. You've missed breakfast, I'm afraid,' said Mo.

'I'm still full up from yesterday. I hope you're not cooking up a storm, Renata. Happy Christmas.' Rachel gathered them both into her arms and hugged them. 'Thank you both for such a tremendous time. I've been waited on and left to sleep, and I feel great.'

Mo brought in a large pot of coffee and they exchanged small, silly gifts. Rachel was delighted with the T-shirt with 'Head Chef' written across it, and Renata beamed at the rainbow-coloured scarf Rachel had bought her, immediately draping it around her head and neck. Mo unwrapped some toronne which Renata had brought from Spain.

'Looks delicious, thank you. I'll open it later.'

'Do you want some cookies to go with your coffee?' asked Renata.

'You're very kind, but I think I'll pass on that, thanks.' Rachel patted her stomach. 'I'm glad we're not having a large meal today, after all your cooking yesterday.'

'That was nothing,' said Renata, waving a hand in the air. 'Just a light lunch today, which I've already started preparing.'

Rachel and Mo exchanged a look and then burst out laughing. 'When do you go home? I swear I will not eat one morsel for at least a month after you've stopped plying us with food,' said Mo.

Renata's face saddened. 'The day after tomorrow is when I leave my new best friends. I am sad to be going, but it will be good to be home for Epiphany. That is when we celebrate Christmas and exchange gifts.'

After declaring Renata's baked fish and tapas scrumptious, Rachel insisted on clearing up, leaving the older women to chat. While she cleaned she thought about Roy and wondered when she would see him again.

8

On Boxing Day, as predicted by Mo, Rachel led her happy, but small, band of workers down the hill to the café.

'I love working here,' said Renata. 'It's such a friendly place. I will take some photos so I can show my friends back home.'

Rachel was pleased she'd opened at the usual time. A number of families came in for hot drinks and cakes. Few sandwiches were filled; everyone probably felt just as stuffed full as she did. Then she heard a muted cough from Renata and looked up.

'Roy? What are you doing here?' Rachel felt Christmas Day had come again.

He smiled. 'I was instructed to turn up, if I remember correctly, isn't that so, Renata?'

She agreed that it had been her idea.

'Can I take your order, sir?' she asked playfully.

'Americano, please.'

'Two Americanos, Mo. Take a seat, sir, and we'll bring them to your table.' Then she glanced at Rachel. 'You can't expect the customer to drink on his own; you must join him. Off you go.'

Rachel and Roy sat at a table by the window and waited for their drinks. They both started talking at once and laughed. 'You first,' said Roy.

'I was just going to ask if you had a good Christmas.'

'It was okay. I always enjoy spending time with the family. How about you? Was yours good?'

'It was full of surprises,' said Rachel. 'The food was awesome — too much of it, of course — and the company couldn't have been better.' Then she thought she'd take a chance and added, 'I enjoyed bumping into you on Christmas Eve.'

He reached over and took her hand lightly in his. 'I enjoyed it, too.'

Then Mo brought the drinks. 'Take your time,' she said. 'As you can see, we're not busy.' Rachel could see she was making a big play of not looking at their joined hands, but it was clear she had noticed them.

'Father Christmas brought you a cashmere scarf, I see,' said Rachel. Its beautiful cobalt-blue colour matched his eyes.

'Chrissie always knows what colours suit me,' he said.

Chrissie? A girlfriend, his wife? Rachel thought immediately. But she was sure he wouldn't be sitting holding her hand if he was involved with someone else. 'Your sister?' she guessed.

He nodded and picked up his cup with his free hand. 'I'm supposed to be carrying all the sales bargains she and Mum are buying.' He drained his coffee quickly and let go of Rachel's hand. 'I still don't know what Renata cooked for you.'

'She's going home tomorrow. I shall be sad to see her go.'

Roy touched Rachel's shoulder gently and kissed the top of her head. Then she heard him chatting to Renata, who clasped him to her and kissed him on both cheeks. He really was a charmer!

★ ★ ★

Rachel and Mo got up at some ungodly hour to bid Renata a safe journey home when the minibus collected her the following morning.

'Will you visit her, do you think?' asked Rachel, filling the kettle and setting out mugs for tea.

Mo nodded. 'Definitely. We got on well.' She bent to get the milk from the fridge. 'Now don't misunderstand me, Rachel, but I think I'd like to have some time spreading my wings a bit. I've thoroughly enjoyed being with you at the café, and it hasn't seemed like work at all. But now you want to take a new direction, and so do I.'

Rachel could hardly believe what she was hearing. She'd relied on Mo very much. Too much? She tried to put her own feelings on hold. This was about Mo. 'You must follow your heart. Go for it, whatever it is.'

'Thanks, Rachel. You're great.'

For a nanosecond, Rachel wondered what would happen if the offer for the property next door wasn't accepted. Would she still close? There would be no choice. On a skeleton staff of two, herself and Mo, it was impossible, so there would be no chance on her own. Things were starting to unravel.

'Time to go,' said Rachel later. 'I'll load my bags into the car. Thanks for letting me stay; it's been a pleasant change.'

'Still missing Michael?' asked Mo.

Rachel shook her head. 'No, I hardly give him a thought. It was pretty mean of him to walk out without a word and to leave the café short-staffed, though.'

'Very unreliable behaviour,' agreed Mo. 'I can't see your Roy doing anything like that.'

Rachel laughed. 'My Roy, eh?'

Perhaps one day he would be.

The start to the day was slow again, but picked up mid-morning, and it was difficult to maintain the level of service which Rachel liked to provide. However, they worked well together and there were no complaints.

'Hi there,' said Mo. 'Can't keep away, it seems. Is it the coffee or the company?'

'I don't need coffee for a buzz at the moment.' Roy came up to the counter, a broad smile plastered on his face. He leaned towards Mo and beckoned Rachel over. 'Nancy was going to phone, but I begged her to let me tell you. I wanted to do it in person.' His eyes were sparkling. 'Mr and Mrs Baxter have accepted your offer if the sale goes through as quickly as possible. They want the past behind them.'

Rachel held her breath and looked at Mo.

'What do you say, Rachel? Shall we move quickly?'

'You're in charge, Auntie.'

'Since when?'

'Since you offered to buy the place.'

They looked down at eight fingers drumming on the counter. 'I can't believe you two!' said Roy. 'Here you are, about to be granted your wish, and you can't make up your minds what to do.'

'Well of course we'll move quickly,' said Mo.

'Definitely,' said Rachel with a nod.

'Good. I'll make a call to the office and set things in motion.' He moved to one side and pulled out his phone.

Rachel and Mo exchanged a high five. 'Great,' said Mo. 'We have a go situation. Now you sit down and I'll bring over drinks and a slice of cake for you and Roy. Quick, while we've got a bit of slack.'

'Thanks for coming over with the news, Roy. It was thoughtful of you. I'm all over the place now. It'll take a while for this to sink in.' Rachel busied herself fiddling with the bits and pieces on the table as she took a bit of time to think. Once her plans moved ahead, there would be no going back. If the restaurant failed, she'd have nothing. Was she doing the right thing?

Roy wiped crumbs from his mouth. 'Can I take you out this evening? A sort of celebration. I have a plan, if you'll trust me.'

'That sounds intriguing. What is it?'

'You'll have to wait and see. It's a surprise. I'll pick you up at your flat around seven if that's all right.'

Rachel nodded. 'Perfect.'

After Roy left, Rachel told Mo her plans for the evening.

'I'll see you tomorrow and expect all the juicy details,' said Mo with a smile.

'If they're juicy, you won't stand a chance of hearing about them,' answered Rachel.

When Rachel arrived home after work, she couldn't wait for seven o'clock. A date with Roy would be fantastic, she felt sure. Nothing could spoil it.

★　★　★

Rachel tensed as she recognised the direction Roy was taking them. It was the village where Michael lived.

'Are you okay?' asked Roy, briefly looking over to her.

'Fine,' she said. 'Are we going far?'

'Nope, we've arrived.' He pulled into the car park of the village hall and stopped the car. 'They're putting on a show here and I thought it might be fun.'

Rachel convinced herself Michael would be nowhere near anything like a village event, but as soon as they walked into the hall he was standing in front of them asking for their tickets.

'Hello, Rachel.' Then he held out his hand to Roy. 'I'm her ex-boyfriend. And you?'

Roy raised his eyebrows at him, ignoring the hand. 'I'm Rachel's *current* man-friend.' He handed over their tickets and led Rachel to the table where they were selling drinks.

'We don't have to stay.' He bent close, his lips tickling her ear.

'I think I'd like to see the show,' she answered. 'And a glass of mulled wine would be nice.'

'I didn't say anything out of place?' asked Roy.

'Like what?'

'Like us being an item.'

'We make a good item. I like you a lot.'

'Me, too. What I mean is, I like you a lot too.'

They giggled, knocked back their small glasses of wine and took their seats as the show began.

Rachel knew right then that she was in love with Roy.

On the way home, Rachel was in a good mood. The show had been funny and very well performed. Roy had held her hand through the performance and they'd chatted during the interval, finding out things about each other. Her attraction to him was growing. In the car, she asked his professional advice as to the merits of letting out her flat.

'It's in a prime position, and the car park is a real plus. I haven't seen the whole flat, of course, but my opinion is that it would command a decent income for you.'

When he named the figure she might get, Rachel nearly keeled over. 'How much? I had no idea.'

'I haven't added in my commission, of course.'

She knew he was teasing, so she countered, 'I'll have to go through Nancy, then. At least she won't swindle me!' Although Rachel hadn't known Roy for long, she knew his integrity was intact and she trusted him implicitly.

Roy pulled up outside her flat and put his arm around Rachel. 'It was great tonight. I hope I dealt with the potential problem at the village hall without making things awkward for you.'

'Michael, he . . . ' started Rachel.

'I don't need the back story,' said Roy. 'I didn't offend you, did I?' She lifted her lips to his cheek, he moved slightly, and they shared a full kiss. When they parted, he said, 'I'll take that as a no.'

'Changing the subject, would you, or someone from your office, come and have a look at the flat? I will definitely consider letting it out.'

'No time like the present,' said Roy, turning to open his door.

'You're kidding! I don't mean now.'

He shrugged. 'It won't take long, and I promise there's no ulterior motive.'

After a professional appraisal of the property, Roy named a slightly higher figure than he'd estimated. Then he picked up the locket which Rachel had meant to wear that evening, but had forgotten. 'This is an interesting piece.' He turned it over and inspected the back. 'May I look inside, or is it personal?'

'There are drawings inside. I have no idea who the people are. It's fascinating. Have a look. I got it at a car boot sale.'

'I love car boot sales.' Roy smiled at

her. Then he turned back to the locket and prised it open with gentle fingers. After a few moments he said, 'They have stories to tell.'

9

MAUD — 1880s

Henry was bored with the constant social events with people he mostly couldn't stand: the women with their simpering ways; and the older men, loud and brash. Even his sisters were annoying him, constantly introducing him to what they thought of as suitable women, potential wives. He knew they and his parents thought he, at twenty-five, should be thinking of marriage, but so far none of the women had taken his fancy. The sooner he was able to get back to London and his more bohemian life, the better.

But for now, his father wanted him at their country residence to learn everything there was to know about it, so he'd be ready to inherit the title and the estate when the time came. The only way he could endure his stay was by regularly riding his horse, Hercules. He wasn't interested in hunting, he preferred taking his time and appreciating the countryside.

Noises from his dressing room alerted him to the fact that it was almost time to get up. The door was ajar, and he watched the maid light the fire, then leave, and a little later return with hot water which she put on the washstand. He hadn't seen the maid before. She had red hair, and wisps which had sprung loose from her cap curled their way round her dimpled cheeks. Her uniform didn't hide her voluptuous figure. As she was about to leave the dressing room, he said, 'Wait! Are you new?'

She jumped. 'Yes, my lord.'

'When did you start?'

'Monday.'

'What's your name?'

'Maud, my lord.'

'Age?'

'Eighteen.'

'Where did you work before?'

'Finchdale Castle, for Baroness Scoleworth. She died, sir. I were dismissed.'

'That formidable woman? She terrified me when I was a child.' He chuckled. 'I knew her well.'

'She were fair, I'll give her that.' She clutched a handful of apron. 'I have to go, my lord, or I'll be in trouble.'

'Yes, yes, go.'

He lay in bed a little longer, wondering about her. 'Maud,' he said out loud. It was a pretty name for a pretty young woman.

★ ★ ★

The next morning, Henry was sitting on the bed when the maid came in.

'Good morning, Maud. How are you today?'

'Very well, thank you, my lord.' She knelt in front of the fireplace and set to work lighting it after opening the shutters.

'It's a lovely day for a brisk walk in

the country.' He liked the way her red hair appeared to be untameable. He'd like to run his hands through it and caress her face.

'I suppose it is. I'll fetch your water.'

He walked to the dressing room and waited for her return. She carefully placed the jug of hot water on the washstand then stood, her head bowed. 'Is that all?'

'Thank you, yes. But wait, your hands, how red and chapped they are.' He lifted her hands gently in his and studied them. 'I have some special ointment which should help. Put it on at night and whenever you get the opportunity.'

'Oh, no, I can't take nothing.'

'You must. Here it is.' He pressed a ceramic pot into her hands. Her face flushed as she hurriedly left the room, stuffing the pot into her pocket as she went.

* * *

Later, as Maud swept the top corridor, she thought about how the young viscount had looked at her. It wasn't so much the way he'd looked at her particularly as the fact that he had even *noticed* her. She, like the other servants, was meant to be invisible, and she always tried hard to blend in with the furniture.

She knew she was lucky to have been given this job. It meant her mother didn't have to worry about keeping her, and she was able to help a little with the family finances. Since the death of her father two years previously, her mother, brothers and sisters had endured great hardship.

That evening, when all the candles had been blown out in her room and she could hear deep breathing coming from the girls in the other two beds, she reached under her pillow for the porcelain pot. Removing the lid, she smelt the ointment. It was lavender-scented, and as she rubbed the soothing balm into her chapped hands, she imagined Henry, as she'd decided to call him in her head, rubbing it in for her.

* * *

Maud looked as if she was daydreaming while she polished the furniture in the bedroom next to his. Henry had been walking along the corridor when he'd seen Maud go into the room. He had silently followed her and had taken the opportunity to observe her.

'How are your hands? Any better?' He moved over to stand in front of her, blocking the doorway.

'Yes, my lord.' She held her arms at her sides.

'May I?' He reached out towards her. She held her hands in front of her and he took them gently and studied them. 'Much better, good. Less than a week and they are almost perfect.'

She took a step backwards. 'I must get on.'

'Of course. I don't want to get you

89

into trouble. But before you get on, tell me, do you like it here?'

'Yes, I do.'

'And what do you do when you are not working?'

'Go to church twice on Sunday. In the evenings we sit in the servants' hall and do our mending.'

'Can you read?'

'Yes, some words.'

'I'll pick a book for you.'

'Thank you.' She scurried from the room.

There was something about her which appealed to him. Although she appeared meek, he felt there was a fieriness under her quiet, calm exterior. He desperately wanted to find out more about her, but he'd need to tread cautiously. She would be dismissed if anyone suspected she was behaving incorrectly.

★ ★ ★

The following day, Henry was up early and searched for Maud, eventually finding her lighting the fire in the drawing room.

'Maud! I have a book for you to read. It's *Black Beauty*. A first edition. At seventeen, I was a little too old for it when it was published, but I read it to my eldest sister's children. It made us all cry, even me.' Maud stood and turned to face him. 'It's extremely sad in parts. Horses are wonderful creatures, and cruelty to them is to be loathed. Now look . . . ' He opened the book. 'See if you can read it.'

She bent her head over the book and studied the page for a while. 'I can make out some of the words. I'd like to try.'

'Here, take it. And if you struggle with any of it, ask me.'

'Thank you.'

He watched as she continued with her work.

She turned and smiled at him. 'Have you nothing better to do than watch a maid set and light a fire?'

He chuckled. 'Nothing at all, not

today. But I will leave you in peace.' He left the room, deciding he would go riding and try to get the woman out of his mind. He had acted inappropriately and must stop himself before any damage was done. Then he remembered her pale skin, the dimples in her cheeks, and the delicate freckles dotting her nose. He barely knew her, and yet there was something about her which attracted him. She had an easy way of movement and a calmness about her work.

★ ★ ★

On Sunday, after church, Henry decided to walk back to Wickwell Hall. It was snowing lightly, and as the snowdrops fell on his lips he licked the iciness away. Walking up the curved drive, he saw a cloaked and hooded figure walking towards him. He knew at once who it was and his heart flipped. 'Maud! I didn't see you in church. Where are you going in these dire conditions?'

'I was working. Now I am going to

see my mother, brothers and sisters. I have the rest of the day off. I should have gone the back way, but it is a long walk even coming down the drive. I must get on, my lord.'

'But it is a shorter ride. You carry on. I will quickly have my horse saddled and will catch up with you. Then we will ride together. What do you say?'

'I must not ride with you.'

'It would be remiss of me to allow you to walk in this weather. Who knows what might happen to you.'

'I can make my own way home.'

'I insist.' He paused. He felt no desire to command her to do as he bid. Strangely, he would prefer to treat her as an equal. 'I am sorry. If you wish to walk, then so be it.'

She smiled. 'I want to travel by horse, but I am afraid we will be seen.'

'I will fetch my horse. We will take care to follow the quietest tracks. I promise no one will recognise us.'

He hurried to the stables, and as soon as Hercules was tacked up, he set off in pursuit of Maud. When he reached her, he leant down and pulled her up to sit in front of him. She laughed as she struggled to get on to the horse, and once she was eventually settled, gave a deep sigh. 'I've never been on a horse before — not a carthorse, nothing. It's so high. Will it throw us off?'

'He is well-behaved and would never throw us off. He follows every command. Walk on.'

As the horse obeyed, Maud leaned back into him. With his arms around her holding the reins, they continued in silence. He felt completely at ease. It was a moment he would treasure.

She directed him to an inn where he said he would remain until she was ready for the return journey.

'Don't wait for me. I can walk, sir.'

'I am here now, and unless you object, we will travel back together on Hercules. Now go and enjoy being with your family.'

★　★　★

94

Before entering the drawing room, Henry took a deep breath. He would be in trouble with his family and knew he had failed in his duties. But the simple pleasure of being with Maud far outweighed any sense of responsibility.

'You are impossible, Henry. Elizabeth was here all afternoon, hoping to see you. You knew she was calling and you went off for hours. She was very upset. Mama is furious. She says you will never get married and she is longing for an heir to the estate.' His sister, Clarice, stopped for breath, but Henry said nothing. 'Where have you been?'

'Riding, drinking and eating at an inn.' He didn't add falling in love.

★ ★ ★

Maud had been given the task of mending bed linen on her return. As she sewed, her thoughts turned to Henry. She'd found him kind, and liked that he'd asked her if she wanted to ride on his horse, rather than telling her she must do so. He was a good-looking man and he dressed handsomely. She knew from talk among the other servants he was in his mid-twenties and was to marry soon, although as far as anyone knew, no suitable wife had been decided upon.

When the footman came downstairs after serving the first course of dinner, he said, 'They're all talking. No raised voices now. The young viscount has his dear mama eating out of his hand again.'

Maud didn't normally listen to gossip about the family, but today she was intrigued.

The footman continued, 'It's possible Lady Elizabeth is the one they want him to marry. She's rich and from a good family. Very beautiful too, and she looks strong enough for childbirth, unlike some of the young women with their delicate ways and fainting fits. Of course, there's no mention of love from those upstairs.'

Having found it impossible to put Henry from her thoughts, she allowed herself to think of their time together, remembering every word, every look, every touch. It delighted her to think he'd spent some of his afternoon with her and had waited for her. As she rubbed the ointment into her hands that night, she thought of Henry's strong hand gripping hers as he'd pulled her on to Hercules. Had the tender look he'd given her when they'd said goodbye meant anything?

10

'We are holding a ball at Christmas, as usual, and Elizabeth will be invited. Don't disappear, Henry.' Lady Hibbledale picked at her food.

'No, Mother. I'll be there and on my best behaviour.' He would have to endure the evening. He didn't want to upset the family.

'You must be attentive to her parents as well as showing some interest in her. I understand she has other suitors.' His mother glared at him.

'We think she'd make you a splendid wife. She has a good temperament, is attractive and has the right connections and breeding,' Lord Hibbledale said.

'She sounds like a horse!'

Henry's sisters tittered at his comment. 'I like her very much,' said Victoria, who at just sixteen longed to be a bridesmaid. 'I'd like my dress to be violet or lilac.'

'I believe it will be Elizabeth who chooses the colour of her attendants' dresses, not you, Victoria,' their mother said.

Henry had endured these discussions before. There had been Margaret, Alice and Rose, all now married, happily he hoped. He wanted just one thing: to love the woman he married. As he sat listening to his family talking about his future, his mind wandered to Maud. He wanted to leave the table and look for her. To tell her that thoughts of her were driving him mad. He must find a way for them to be together. Was it futile? Of course it was, he told himself. There was no possibility of Maud, a housemaid, being the mistress of Wickwell Hall. He must forget her.

★   ★   ★

As Maud made her way up the back stairs to her attic bedroom, she was surprised when Henry suddenly appeared in front of her.

'You scared me, my lord.' She clutched her skirt. 'Why are you here? The family do not use the back stairs.'

'I'm sorry I alarmed you. I haven't seen you for a while, and I wanted to make sure you were all right.'

'Another maid sees to your fire and water. There is talk you are to wed Lady Elizabeth, so you must be very happy.'

'You're wrong!' He leaned against the wall. 'What am I to do? I have no interest in Elizabeth. It's you, Maud, I want to get to know. Ever since I first met you, my mind has been consumed by you. I think of you when I wake up and when I go to sleep. I think of you all day long. You are driving me mad!'

'I don't mean to.' She was shocked. She'd had no idea he harboured such strong feelings for her.

'Of course you don't. Oh, Maud.' He took her hands in his and raised them to his lips. 'It is you I want to dance with at the ball, it is you I want to fetch delicacies for, it is you I want to toast with champagne.'

She wanted to take him in her arms and kiss his face, his cheeks, his eyes, his mouth.

He reached forward, took her face in his hands and put his lips to hers, gently at first and then more intensely. She kissed him back with a passion.

That night, after brushing her hair, she took his book from under the mattress and sat on the edge of the bed. She'd tried to read it, but her schooling had been short and she struggled with most of the words. She ran her fingers over the green cloth cover and felt the embossed gold and black detailing. She sighed. She, a servant, had fallen in love with the heir of Wickwell Hall, and it appeared he had fallen in love with her. There was nothing to be done.

★ ★ ★

Any glimpse she had of Henry filled her heart with joy. Occasionally he would meet her gaze and smile furtively. It was impossible to be rid of the strong emotions she felt. If only he was of her class, or she of his. She had seen the beautiful Lady Elizabeth arriving at the Hall. Everything about her was elegant: the way she held herself, her clothes, her hair and make-up. In time, Henry would be sure to fall in love with her, and she, a lowly maid, would be forgotten. She listened to the gossip in the servants' hall.

'I think Lady Elizabeth is perfect for him. They spent yesterday afternoon together in the drawing room, heads together looking at some book or other. That's what I overheard Mr Jenkins saying,' Bertha, Maud's friend, said.

The cook came to the doorway. 'Enough gossip, Bertha. I want you in the kitchen now. There are vegetables to be peeled and bread to be made. We haven't got all day.'

★   ★   ★

Henry was finding his time in the country difficult. He wanted to be near

Maud, to get to know her better. But he barely saw her, and when he did they couldn't talk. His mother and sisters were forever finding an entertainment where Lady Elizabeth was included, and she, poor woman, was showing signs of falling in love with him, although he couldn't understand why. It was mean and uncalled for, but he tended to be brusque with her. He knew his duty, had known it practically all his life. He was the heir, must marry suitably and have children. Although he enjoyed the benefits of his position, he sometimes wished his life was more ordinary. He wouldn't mind doing hard manual work to provide for a wife and children. A simple life was appealing in many ways.

Maud, with her lack of airs and graces, her sweet simplicity, was who he wanted. He imagined leading her by the hand into the drawing room and introducing her to his parents as his intended. The consequences were unthinkable.

★ ★ ★

On an errand for the butler, Mr Jenkins, to deliver a package to an old family retainer, Maud was startled when she was suddenly grabbed from behind and held tightly.

'Got you!' Henry spun her round. 'I haven't seen you for days. It's been unbearable. I've waited in corridors, hidden round corners, and haven't once come across you. I've missed you.'

Maud stared into his cornflower-blue eyes and reached to touch his unruly dark hair. He had fine well-proportioned features, and she delighted in his smile. They kissed briefly, then he grabbed her hand. 'Come on, I know a place we can go.'

She pulled back. 'I can't. I have to deliver this parcel and get back to the Hall.'

'I'll make an excuse for you. I'll say you were accosted by a handsome stranger.'

She laughed. 'No, I really, can't.'

'When can I see you, then? I have to see you.'

'P'raps Sunday afternoon. If I am able to leave the Hall, I'll meet you behind the stable.'

★   ★   ★

Henry waited. He could hear the horses moving about in the stable, and occasionally one of them whinnied. It was a cold January day, and he stamped his feet to keep warm. His breath misted the air. Footsteps approached; light, delicate footsteps. Then Maud appeared from around the corner. They fell into each other's arms.

He led her into the stables to a stall laid with fresh straw. 'This is ready for a purchase of my father's, a new pony for Victoria. It arrives tomorrow.' He knelt down and patted the straw. 'Shall we sit here?'

They sat together, leaning back on the wooden partition, their hands intertwined.

'It's wonderful to be close to you again,' he murmured.

She smiled and turned her head to

kiss him. He knew he should stop this folly, but he was powerless to fight his feelings for her. As their lips met it was as though he was drowning in her love. Forced on by desire, they tried to keep their lips upon each other's as they tore at clothing, throwing it in wild abandon until at last they lay naked. Then they hungrily satisfied their desire before lying in each other's arms.

Later, Henry brushed straw from Maud's skirt and helped button her blouse. Her face was flushed, but she smiled serenely at him. He could hear the horses in the other stalls moving about, restless knowing people were near.

'What now, Henry?' she asked.

'Now I have to find a way for us to be together.' They kissed tenderly and left the stables separately to return to their detached lives.

★　★　★

That night, after she had finished her duties at the Hall, Maud thought of what they'd done in the stables. She knew it would seem wrong in other people's eyes, but to her it was perfect and natural. They loved each other, and surely showing that love was right. She hugged herself and pictured Henry's smiling face. Somehow they would find a way to be together. He'd said so, hadn't he?

11

The year progressed, and Henry's time at the Hall was coming to an end. Soon he would return to London. He would miss riding in the country and he would miss Maud.

A knock at his bedroom door startled him. 'Enter.' He hoped it was Maud. She had occasionally secretly managed to come to his room.

'Henry.' She rushed across to him. She looked paler than usual, and her eyes were red as though she'd been crying.

'Whatever is the matter?' He took her in his arms. 'If you are upset that I am leaving to go back to London, do not worry. I am thinking of a way to take you with me. What do you say to that? We will be together in the house in London.'

Maud wiped her face with her apron.

'I can't come with you. I must go home to my family.' She shook her head. 'The shame of it.'

'Shame? What shame? There is no shame in true love. And why will you tell them now, before we have decided what to do?'

'I am not going to tell them about you . . . about us. I am going to tell them I'm having a baby. It is your child, Henry.'

Dear Lord, what had he done? Maud was going to have his child, maybe a son, and now he would have to deal with the consequences. He walked over to the chair by the fire and sank into it.

'What are we to do? This is disastrous,' he said.

'Not for you. You need have nothing to do with it. It would be for the best.' Her voice sounded strangely sad.

He didn't know what to say. He had known the potential consequences of the snatched moments he'd had with Maud, but somehow it was still a shock.

'Downstairs, they say your marriage

to Lady Elizabeth is to happen and soon,' she sobbed.

He wanted to put his arms around her and tell her everything would be all right, but he'd been naïve. There was no possibility of being with Maud and her child — their child. He would be disinherited, and then what would he have? What would he be?

He was lost in thought when Maud said, 'Say something, please, Henry. Do you not care for me? Give me some words of love as you have done so many times.'

He had never heard her raise her voice before, his sweet gentle Maud. He took her in his arms. 'Maud, you are angry, but you must realise I cannot bring up your child as mine. It is impossible. I love you, of course I do. But I am shocked at your announcement. It is unexpected, and difficult for me to know what to do and say.'

'You don't have to do anything. I am going home. I will bring shame to my family, but we will survive. And you needn't worry that I will tell anyone who the father of my child is. We want nothing from you. I will bring up my child to be honest and true. Be sure of that.' Tears streamed down her face. She turned her back on him and left the room, slamming the door behind her.

He sat on the bed and rubbed his face with his hands. What a fool he'd been. To think he could fall in love with a maid, someone from the lower classes. He *did* love her, and would never forget her pretty face and unruly red hair. He wondered if their child would have a fiery streak. *Stop it*, he told himself. *I must not think of the child. I must forget Maud; and if she was willing to go away with no fuss, that was for the best.*

★   ★   ★

Love tokens. That was what she'd seen them as. She stared at the objects on the bed and picked them up one by one. She took the lid off the empty ceramic pot and inhaled the lingering fragrance. How kind she'd thought him when he'd given her the ointment. The book, which unless he asked for it, she would never return. And between the back cover and the last page, some pressed flowers. They had been tokens of love, that was for sure. One day he'd given her a tiny posy and told her the forget-me-nots were for true love and the spray of fern for sincerity. She should get rid of them, but she'd treasured them and would continue to do so, along with their child. She put them all away carefully and sat on the bed. She had decided she would work at the Hall for as long as she could. As soon as her condition started to show, she would tell them she was leaving. Dealing with her sickness in the mornings was something she would have to hide from everyone. It would be difficult, but her family needed her small earnings and she must work for as long as possible.

Her mother hadn't taken the news well, and the thought of one more mouth to feed, as well as the gossip in the village, had worried her.

'You'll have to leave the baby with me once it's old enough and you've found yourself a new position. I'll bring it up as one of my own. Paul is barely eight; they'll be close enough.'

'No, I'm not leaving my baby. And I'm not going to get a good reference, what with only being at Wickwell Hall a short time and not giving much notice.' Maud brushed her hair from her face.

'There's no future for you, then. No decent man is going to want to marry you, and there isn't much work locally. I don't know what we'll do. Your poor father will be turning in his grave. And you say the child's father is one of the servants. We won't get much help from him, then.' She angrily kneaded the dough and set it to prove before wiping her flour-covered hands on her apron.

Maud hadn't wanted to lie to her mother, but if she told her the truth she would want to contact Henry and ask for some help. Maud wanted nothing more to do with him. She had loved him and he had abandoned her when she had most needed him. But she wouldn't abandon her child, no matter how hard it proved to be.

'It's going to be a difficult time for us, Maud, but I'll help as best I can. It's all right for those people in their castles and manors, eating their delicacies and dressed in their finest. I hear from the farrier that the son and heir at Wickwell Hall is courting Lady Elizabeth, from one of the richest families in England. *She'll* never have to worry about where her next meal is coming from.'

Maud had felt sick. She'd known about Henry's future. He was to marry Lady Elizabeth. But it pained her to think such a little time had passed since she'd told him about their baby.

'We mustn't think of that. We must count our blessings and do the best we can,' she had said.

But now after walking out of the back entrance of Wickwell Hall for the last time, she had to stop and lean against the wall. A sob escaped her and she breathed deeply. Henry was in London and wouldn't know or care that she was leaving that day. Taking another deep breath, she told herself everything would be all right. She placed a hand gently on the barely visible mound of her stomach. She would give her child a good life and bring him up to be a decent person. Holding her head high, she walked down the drive and away from the father of her child, the man she had loved with all her heart.

* * *

It wasn't easy to manage. While her mother worked at the large farm just outside the village, Maud looked after her younger brothers and sisters, took in washing and repaired bed linen and clothing. She tired easily, and by the end of each day was ready for her bed, although sharing with two of her sisters didn't make for a restful night. Her mother was always tired too, but one day came home full of excitement.

'Pour me a cup of tea, Maud; I'm parched. They work me hard up at the farm, but today Mrs Smith was very talkative. It seems their eldest son, Edgar, is coming back tomorrow and is going to be helping his father on the farm. I told you he's been in Wales staying with some relatives who have a farm there.'

'It won't make any difference to us, will it?'

'It could, my girl, it certainly could.'

Maud sat at the kitchen table and rubbed her back. She looked across at her mother. 'It's a mystery to me.'

'He'll be looking for a wife! And being the eldest son, he'll take over the farm. He'll be well set up.'

'It's on Lord Hibbledale's estate, which means they are tenants of Lord Hibbledale.' Maud put her hand over her mouth. She mustn't say any more and let slip the name of her baby's father.

'I can't see that's anything to do with it. You and the child would be comfortable, and you could take on your brothers and sisters in the house or on the farm. Maybe two or three of them could live in.'

'I can see how eager you are, but why would Edgar be interested in a fallen woman? *And* I remember him as being a dirty, scruffy man and rather bad-mannered. Would you wish that on me?' Maud picked at a scratch in the table.

'I suppose you think you could marry the lord of the manor. Would his lordship, Henry, suit you? I'll see what I can arrange.'

Tears welled in Maud's eyes. Yes, he would have suited her quite well. And because of her love for him, her mother would marry her to someone she could barely look at without a feeling of disgust. She stood and walked over to stir the stew. It was mainly root vegetables and little meat. She imagined the meals they ate at the farm and wished Edgar was someone she could feel attracted to. She longed to make things better, but she'd dearly loved once and anything else wouldn't be enough.

12

'It's a girl.' Her mother beamed as she handed Maud the baby wrapped in a white shawl.

Maud held her closely and gazed at the tiny face and little hand poking out. 'Hello, Anna,' she whispered, letting her finger be grasped.

'Is that what you're going to call her? Anna. It's a pretty name, but not one used in this family.'

'I just like it.' Maud thought of the book which she'd hidden with her other treasures in the trunk. She pulled the shawl from her baby's head and stroked the downy hair. 'I wonder if she'll have red hair like me.'

'She may turn out like her father. Good-looking, was he?'

'Don't start, not now. I've told you I

will never give away his name, not to you or anyone. Not to Anna. He's the past and this little one is the future. I have to do my best for her.'

'I've been thinking about that. In a few months it will be hay-making at the farm. They'll need extra help, and by then the baby will be old enough for us to manage her between us. I'm going to take over the washing, mending and chores here; I have too many aches and pains to be doing the heavy work at the farmhouse. You rest now.' She bundled up the soiled linens and left the room.

Maud knew she would have to work on the farm, as there was little other work to be had. Meanwhile, she would treasure Anna.

★   ★   ★

The kitchen was silent as Maud sat at the table, her head bowed over a sheet of paper, chewing the end of a pencil. What should she write? Henry and Elizabeth were betrothed, but that was nothing to do with her. She had to write to him, though, to finish what had been started, once and for all. She knew he was back at the Hall, so she had to do it now.

'Paul,' she called out to her young brother, who was out in the yard playing with some stones and a few marbles, 'you are a clever boy and I have a job for you, but it must be a secret between you and me. You mustn't say anything to Mother or to anyone else. Do you understand?' He nodded, and his hair flopped forward. She pushed it away from his face. 'Do you know who the eldest son of Lord Hibbledale is?'

'He is called Henry, although we mustn't call him that, and I have seen him riding his horse a way over there.' He pointed vaguely.

'But would you know him if you saw him again?'

'He rides almost every day.'

'And you are sure it is he?'

'I am.'

'Tomorrow you are to wait for him and give him this letter. Only if he is alone. Ask him first if he is the Earl of Hibbledale's eldest son, Henry. You must be sure it is Henry you give the letter to, no one else.'

'I can do that.'

'I know you can. And you will get a reward. I will get you some humbugs.' He had a sweet tooth and she would find a way to buy him a few.

'Humbugs! I will keep your secret.'

★   ★   ★

Henry was enjoying his ride. Hercules was on good form, and after cantering as far as the woods, he was now trotting gently. It felt good to be alive. Elizabeth was besotted, and he enjoyed the attention she gave him. He didn't love her, probably never would, but as a marriage of convenience it would suit him very well. He would canter across the next field and leap the brook.

Just as Hercules was gathering pace,

a child leapt out in front of them, causing the horse to rear and almost unseat him. Once he had calmed Hercules and was back in control, he glared at the child. 'Silly little fool! What are you playing at?'

'I'm not playing, my lordship, my lord, Sir Henry. You are Henry, the eldest son of the Earl of Hibbledale?'

It was as though he was repeating something he'd been told to say. 'I am, but who wants to know?'

'My sister, Maud. She said if I give you this letter in secret, she will buy me some humbugs.'

Maud had sent him a letter. No doubt asking for something for the baby. He had calculated it would be born about now. His heart pounded.

With trembling fingers, he unfolded the sheet and read the looped writing.

Dear Henry,

I am writing to tell you that sadly our daughter died soon after birth. There is no need to worry that you will ever be found out. I have told no one.

I wish you are happy when you marry the lady.
Maud

When he had finished, he tucked it in his jacket pocket and closed his eyes. He'd had a daughter and never seen her. Tears formed and he let them trickle down his cheeks. Poor Maud, how she must have suffered. He pictured her face and the way she'd flicked her luxuriant red hair after they'd made love. He remembered her lively spirit and her dimpled cheeks. She was a good woman, saying she would tell no one and wishing him well in spite of her grief.

★　★　★

Henry thought he might be less conspicuous if he walked to the village to find Maud. Weeks had passed since he'd received the letter. As he neared the first houses, an elderly man doffed his cap. 'G'day, my lord.'

'Good morning. I wonder if you can help me. I am looking for a woman called Maud. A message was to be brought to her and I required a walk so offered to find her.'

'She's out hay-making. Look yonder.' The man pointed to a field, golden with hay, figures busily moving about.

'Thank you.' Henry walked over to the field and stopped in the shadow of the hedge. Maud looked well, healthier than when she'd worked the long hours at the Hall. Her hair was tied back under a scarf, but it was long and hung down her back. Her beautiful hair. She was laughing with another woman. He wondered how she appeared so happy so soon after the heartbreak of losing a baby. He felt in his pocket for the velvet bag which he would give her.

'Maud,' he called.

She didn't hear, but her friend did and said something to her. She looked up, and shading her eyes with her hands, walked over to him. Her face was no longer pale and her freckles were darker than previously. The sun now kissed her where once he had.

'Henry! Why are you here? There will be talk.'

'I had to see you. I am very sorry the baby died.'

'Let us go to the other side of the hedge. I don't want the others watching us.'

He followed her. He had known it was foolish to come. 'What did you name her?'

'Anna, after the author of *Black Beauty*. But don't torment yourself. Everything has turned out for the best. You are to be wed and will be happy.'

Henry took the velvet bag from his pocket and offered it to her. 'It is a mourning locket. I would like you to have it.' He pushed it into her hands. 'Do you have a lock of Anna's hair?'

She nodded.

'Then please put it in the locket with the pictures I have drawn, then the three of us will be together forever. I'm very sorry, Maud, for what has happened. Please always remember I did love you, but circumstances . . . '

'I know. Now go.' She wiped her tears away before heading back to her work.

★ ★ ★

Once home, she went upstairs and tipped out the contents of the velvet bag into her hand. It was a beautiful locket with lily of the valley on the front and an engraving of a church on the back. She carefully prised open the locket, and inside were two portraits drawn in pen and ink. One was a self-portrait of Henry and the other was of her. He had caught their likenesses. She had cut some of Anna's hair when the baby had been just a few days old, so took a small amount and inserted it under her picture, as promised. Then she tucked the locket in the bottom of the trunk where she kept her other treasures.

She felt happy Henry had acknowledged their child, but she also knew he would be no part of her life. Edgar had shown an interest in her over the past few weeks in spite of her having carried a child out of wedlock. The more she came to know him, the more she liked him. He had started to take care of his appearance, and once he'd had his hair cut and had trimmed his beard, she found him almost handsome. But that was of no importance. He'd become kind and was good to his workers. Maud looked forward to her days on the farm and the chance of spending time with him.

13

It seemed a short time since she and Edgar had married, but looking at their brood sitting at the table enjoying Sunday dinner, Maud thought of the years which had passed. They now had one girl and three boys. The oldest child, Anna, was thirteen and enjoyed helping Edgar on the farm. They had been blessed. It was sad her mother had died the previous year, but she was happy Paul and two of her other brothers worked on the farm. Sometimes when she was working at her household tasks, she thought of Henry and wondered if he was happy. His father had died and he was now the Earl of Hibbledale, but she'd heard he rarely stayed at his country estate. She had also heard that Elizabeth, his wife, had been unable to carry babies full term and had lost several. She hoped

Henry loved his wife.

She felt her stomach as the child moved inside her.

'Let us have a song, Maud,' Edgar said.

Maud was happy, surrounded by her family. Life could not have turned out better for her.

★   ★   ★

Anna could barely listen to the screams coming from the bedroom upstairs. The baby was arriving early and she had been told by Mrs Collins, who helped all the village women when they gave birth, to fetch hot water and more towels. Her father was out working, but she'd sent for him. No one else was in the house. She'd been around when her brothers had been born, but none had seemed like this. Her mother was in agony and Anna bit her top lip as she listened. It was late afternoon and the pains had started in earnest in the morning.

She hurried upstairs with the water, then fetched towels from a cupboard on the landing. When her mother recognised her standing by the bed, she gripped her hand. Sweat had soaked her hair and her face glistened. Mrs Collins wiped her forehead with a cloth.

'Anna, if anything happens, look after your father and the children. Don't let the family fall apart.' Her face contorted and she let out a cry of anguish.

'No, Mother. But you're going to be all right, don't worry.' She heard a door bang downstairs and rushed down to tell her father what was happening.

'Go back to her, Anna. She'll need you with her.' His face was grey and he slumped into a chair.

Back in the room, Mrs Collins beckoned her over to the dresser. 'I couldn't save him.' She pointed at the small baby wrapped in a blanket. 'We must look after your mother.'

The night was long, but by the morning Maud was a better colour and slept peacefully.

'I think she's going to pull through, Father,' she said at breakfast.

'I hope so. I'm going to sit with her today. I will leave you to oversee the others and the farm. Make sure the essential jobs are done, but try to have a rest later. You've been up all night.'

Anna watched him leave the room.

A howl from upstairs alarmed her. It was a man's voice, but the sound was like none she'd heard before. She ran up the stairs and into her parents' room. Her father was leaning over her mother, speaking through his sobs.

'You can't leave me. I love you.' He put her hand to his lips and kissed it, then reached over and kissed her forehead, her cheeks and her lips.

Anna walked over and put her hand on his shoulder. Her mother's body was lifeless and her eyes stared up at her. She gently closed her eyelids. How had this happened? And then she saw the blood. What had gone wrong? She didn't know what to do or say. How would they manage without her? She

132

made the decision immediately. She would leave school now, and even when she was old enough to marry and move away, she would stay at home and look after her family to ensure it didn't fall apart, just as her mother had asked.

★   ★   ★

Her father didn't argue with her decision, and as the school leaving age was thirteen, she was allowed to. She was needed at home. After the funeral, and when they were all getting accustomed to their mother not being around, her father told her he had a task for her.

'I'd like you to sort through your mother's belongings. Make sure nothing is wasted. Her clothes can be altered or made into things for the rest of us. There are things in the trunk which I know were precious to her, but I've never looked at them. I'll leave you to decide what's to be done with it all.'

'Of course I'll do that.'

She started with the clothes. As she

handled the items, she held them to her face and breathed in the distinctive fragrance. Her mother hadn't possessed a lot, but there were things she could wear and some she could make clothes and cleaning cloths from.

Next, the trunk. Carefully she lifted the lid and looked inside. There wasn't much. A few bits and pieces she and her siblings had made when they'd been younger. There was a picture of the whole family drawn by Michael, her youngest brother. Under the papers she found a book, *Black Beauty* by Anna Sewell. It had a beautiful cover, green embossed in black and gold. Inside the cover were pressed flowers. There was a small lidded porcelain pot. She looked inside. It was empty. She wondered if these were love tokens from her father. A velvet bag was tucked in the corner. She undid the drawstring and tipped out the contents onto the bed. It was a locket on a bracelet. Barely able to breathe, she opened the locket and found two drawings of a young woman and a man, along with a lock of fine, downy hair. The woman was clearly her mother, but the man was not at all like her father. Had this man been her mother's sweetheart at one time? And why was the locket on a mourning bracelet? Had the man died? Who was he? She could ask her father, but it was possible he knew nothing about this man.

Days passed as she wondered what story the objects in the trunk were hiding. Her sadness at the loss of her mother deepened and she decided she would read the book to feel closer to her. After settling on her bed, as the gas light flickered making shadowy shapes on the walls and ceilings, she turned the first pages. On the title page was a faint name in pencil. Anna held the book up closer to the light. 'Henry' was the name, and then it read 'Wickwell Hall'. Her mind somersaulted. The book was a fine one. Who at Wickwell Hall would possess this book and give it to her mother? She wracked her brain. The present earl hardly ever came to the estate, but what was his name? Was it Henry? Surely not. How would her mother have known the earl? Before she married her father, she'd been a maid at the Hall, but just a lowly maid. Her mother had never wanted to talk about her life there. How was she to solve the puzzle of the items?

★   ★   ★

Several months had passed since the death of her mother, but Anna missed her every day and their father had become weaker, not just physically, but in the way he used his authority around the farm. Anna was busy finishing the last of the ironing when Michael rushed in.

'I've just seen the earl going by. He's got a new motor car. It goes really fast. Like this.' He whooshed round the room pretending his hand was the car.

'Was he going to or away from the Hall?'

'To the Hall. He's come for the summer. With the countess. One of my

136

friends told me.'

After folding the last item of clothing, she put the book, jar and locket into a bag. 'Michael, I'm going out. I won't be long. When the others come in, tell them dinner is in the oven. Meantime, behave yourself.'

'Where are you going?'

'I have an errand. I'll be back soon.' With that, she pulled off her apron and left the house. As she walked, she wondered how she was going to get past the servants to see the earl. What could she say or do?

She went to the back door and tapped on it before stepping inside. The butcher was just leaving, and the woman she imagined was the cook was seeing him out.

'Yes? Can I help you?' The woman looked her up and down.

'I need to speak to the earl.'

'And I need to speak to the queen. Is it a job you want? We're overstaffed as it is.'

'No. Would you make sure he gets

this book and say Maud's daughter, Anna, is returning it? Please.'

The cook took the book and turned it over. 'It's a fine book. How did you come by it?'

'It's a long story and not one I fully understand. I think the earl will want to meet me when he sees it.'

'I'll do what I can. Luckily, he's a good-tempered man. Wait outside the back door.'

Anna went out and leant against the wall, holding her face up to the sun. She closed her eyes and was startled when she felt a tap on her arm.

'He wants to see you,' the cook said. 'You must come in this way. One of the maids will show you up to the drawing room.'

The maid knocked on a panelled door and opened it before standing back to let Anna in.

'Come in, come in. And sit down. Let's have no formality.' The earl gestured at a chair. 'How did you come by this book?'

'It was in my mother's trunk. She was called Maud.'

'Was? What do you mean, was?'

'She died in childbirth.'

'She was a young woman in her thirties. How could she die?' He walked over to the large window and stared out into the garden. 'Poor thing. Did the child survive?'

'No, he died too.'

'Another dead baby, poor Maud. I knew her well when she worked here.' He turned and walked back towards her. 'What did you come for?'

'My father asked me to sort her things out after she died. I found the book, along with — ' he reached into the bag and pulled out the locket. 'This, and this pot. I saw your name in the book and I wondered how my mother came by it.'

'I gave her the book as a gift. It pleases me that she kept it, treasured it even. The maid said your name is Anna. Strange she should use the same name for another daughter.'

'I'm sorry, my lord, but I have no idea what you are saying.'

'Of course you don't; it was before you were born. How old are you?'

'Nearly fourteen.'

He stared at her. 'That can't be right. It's not possible.' He slumped in a chair and rubbed his forehead with his hand. 'I can't believe it.'

'Believe what?' She hoped he wasn't ill. His face had turned white.

'That you are alive.'

'Of course I'm alive.' Now she wondered if there was something wrong with him. Maybe she should leave before he said anything else strange.

He stared at her as though he was taking in every detail of her features. It was disturbing.

'You are very like your mother. The pale skin, the fiery red hair.'

They sat in silence for a while and she felt uncomfortable. 'I've returned your book, so I'll go now. Although maybe this is yours too.' She held the locket out to him, but he didn't take it.

'No, it's your mother's. I gave it to her when she let me know her daughter had died. Our daughter.' He smiled at her. 'Maud had such lovely wavy red hair. As do you.'

'I don't understand what you're saying. You and she had a daughter who died?'

'She told me you'd died. But your age tells me our daughter lives. You are my daughter, Anna. I am your father.'

'No! My father is at home.' Her heart pounded and she felt breathless. Her world was spinning. She leant back in the chair.

'Your father is here in this room with you. And I thought I would never have a child. My wife and I have been unfortunate and she is unable to carry them to term. It is impossible to believe that you are here in the room with me. My daughter, Anna.' He sighed.

It had been a mistake to bring the book back. The earl was quite mad. How could she be his daughter when she already had a father?

'I am overjoyed to meet you, Anna. Let me explain.' He reached for her hands and told her about his time with her mother. 'Why do you think she told me you were dead? To free me for my predestined life?'

'To free you? You mean so that you could get married and have your own family without the burden of me?' Anna was confused. She'd spent a lifetime believing Edgar to be her father, and now this man, the earl, said *he* was her father.

'You can't imagine how delighted I am. I will help you in any way I can, although we will have to keep this from my wife.'

'I don't want anything from you, and I won't tell anyone. All I wanted was to know why the book and locket were special to Mother, and now I do. I will leave you.' She felt like running away and hiding.

'We must see each other. Now that we know of each other, I don't want to lose you again. I want to help you. I can give you money.'

Anna took a deep breath. 'No. For years you have believed me dead. Continue to do so. I realise why Mother did what she did, and I have been disloyal to her by coming here, although that wasn't my intention.'

He knelt down in front of her and took her hands in his. 'However you feel and whatever you think, please remember that I loved her with all my heart and I believe she loved me.'

'I am sorry for you both, but Mother was happy with my father.'

'I am glad she at least had a happy, if short, life. I made a terrible mistake when I didn't fight to be with her, when I put my position and reputation above my love for her. It was wrong and I have paid the price. I have had an unhappy life with my wife.' He sighed before continuing, 'You say you don't want anything, but please let me give you something. Some small thing. Books. I will give you some books. They bring great joy. You can read?'

'Quite well, but I am keen to improve.'

'I will send a box of books to you.'

Anna felt sorry for the man. He was desperate to do something for her, and sending her a box of books appeared to please him. She wouldn't argue. Somehow she would explain their arrival at the farm to her father. But now she must leave the earl.

★　★　★

Henry didn't move. He sat in the drawing room trying to remember how he'd felt when he'd been with Maud, closing his eyes to try and conjure up every detail of her face and to imagine her laughter. She had laughed a lot, something Elizabeth rarely did. If only they'd had a chance to be together. And now she was dead. But their daughter lived. Joy bubbled inside him. He couldn't publicly acknowledge her, but surely he could see her occasionally and ensure she was well cared for. He would find out more about the man she called her father, and he would certainly offer her family work on the estate if they needed it. He would remain in the background, but keep his eye on his only daughter.

★　★　★

Anna was dreading facing her father and asking him questions about the past. Devastated that he wasn't her real father, she didn't know what to say to him. All she could hope was that he knew the truth and didn't believe she was his daughter.

Once in the parlour, she sat down opposite her father. 'I have just discovered that you are not my father.'

He didn't look shocked and simply said, 'I see.'

'Is there nothing else to say?'

'I've loved you like my own. Isn't that enough?'

'You have been a good father, better than most. But I think I should know the truth. I believe I am the earl's daughter.'

'Yes, you are. Your mother was unmarried when she gave birth to you, but she came to work here on the farm and we fell in love. We married and decided we'd bring you up as my daughter. Everyone else in the village accepted it as a good thing, and with time no one thought or spoke about it. Your mother loved the earl and she believed he loved her. But there was no possibility he could marry a maid. After you were born, she decided it would be best if he thought you'd died so that there would be no contact between them. It enabled us to live happily as a family without interference. Your mother was a good woman, and she braved the shame of having an illegitimate child in this small community. You should be proud of her. Don't harbour bad feelings towards her.'

'I don't. But I wish *you* were my father. I feel desolate that it is a stranger.'

'It has made no difference to me and

it should make none to you. You are my daughter and will be until the day I die.'

With that Anna burst into tears, and Edgar quickly took her into his arms and held her.

* * *

Anna had done what she'd promised her mother and stopped the family from falling apart. With all her brothers working away from home except Michael, she was restless. At twenty-three, Anna felt it was time for her to do something new. All she'd ever done was look after the family and help on the farm. She had read about the Voluntary Aid Detachments being formed and wondered if there was any way she would be accepted for training.

'What do you think, Father? As far as I can tell, it is women from the middle and upper classes who are being taken on, and I am just the daughter of a maid.'

'Of an earl, Anna. If you have set

your heart on this, go and see his lordship and ask him to help.'

'I can't. Supposing his wife heard about it? I don't want to ruin his marriage.'

'There you go again, thinking of everyone else except yourself. I've heard he's here with his sisters and their families. The countess stayed in London. It's said she doesn't care for the country.'

For days she pondered the idea, but she desperately wanted to volunteer. She put on her cloak and boots and set off for the hall. She was fortunate to find the earl at the back of the house outside the stables.

He walked over to her. 'Anna! How lovely to see you. Come into the house. My sisters and their daughters are out. What a wonderful surprise.'

He seemed genuinely happy, but Anna couldn't get it out of her mind that his sisters and nieces were her aunts and cousins. It was very strange to have a family she didn't know.

He led her into the drawing room and offered her a chair. 'Let's have tea.' He rang the bell for the maid, and after she'd left the room, he asked, 'And what may I do for you?'

'I would like to join the Voluntary Aid Detachment in town and learn first aid and nursing. I have my father's permission.'

'You do.'

'I meant Edgar's permission, my true father.' She blushed. It was difficult, as she didn't want to dishonour Edgar or upset his lordship.

'You'd like me to put a word in for you? As it happens, my nieces are training there at the moment. You could travel in with them.'

'But what will we tell people?'

'It doesn't matter what people think. Your mother knew that.'

14

When war broke out, Anna's brothers — John, Robert and Michael — immediately joined the army, much to her distress. She was particularly concerned about Michael, who at just twenty seemed too young to be going to fight.

'What about me, Father? What can I do?' She longed to support the young men going to war.

'You must do what you've been training for. That is why the Voluntary Aid Detachments were created, so that people are trained and ready to help the war effort. I hear the Red Cross are setting up a hospital in the church hall in Hincham Bridge.'

Helping the sick and wounded came easily to her, and after her initial embarrassment helping men to undress, wash and dress, she soon overcame it.

As she and one of the other young

women, Ida, were giving a patient a bed bath, they shared what they'd overheard on the wards.

'It seems we aren't wanted overseas. Apparently most of the civilian women volunteers are not used to hardship and hospital discipline,' Ida said.

'That's true enough. But some of us could do the work. Would you want to go to another country and face all that danger?'

'I've never been *anywhere*.' Ida laughed. 'It would be a proper adventure.'

'But dangerous.'

'Our boys are facing danger. Why shouldn't we?'

★ ★ ★

Before she left for France, Anna decided she would visit the earl. She'd heard he was busy turning the Hall into a convalescent home for wounded soldiers. As she walked up the driveway, she felt a sense of neglect. A man opened the back door when she knocked.

'I'd like to see the earl, please. Tell him Anna is here.'

When the man led her to her father in one of the bedrooms, he was moving a bed with the help of a young maid.

'Anna! How good to see you. I was going to visit you. We're rearranging the furniture, but let's go downstairs. It's time for a rest.' He kissed her cheek, took her by the hand and escorted her down the stairs to the drawing room. 'I'll ring for someone to bring us tea. It's not like the old days. Jenkins, the butler, is still here and a few young maids, but all the young men have gone to war. Times are changing. Life for many of us will never be the same again. We will never get back to how things were before the war started,' Henry said.

'I'm sure we will. Everything will be normal, just as it was. The Hall will be a grand house again and you will be surrounded by your loyal servants.' She didn't believe what she was saying. The normal they had known was gone.

'The reason I was going to visit you was because Wickwell Convalescent Home is going to be staffed mainly by VADs and I'd like you to be one of them,' he said.

'How kind of you to think of me, but I'm afraid I have other plans. I am going to France. At last we've been accepted to work overseas.'

'Why put yourself in danger when your skills are required by the wounded being sent back from the battlefields?'

'Because I am needed *there*.'

'You have your mother's determination! I will worry about you until you are safely home again. Is there no way I can dissuade you?'

'None at all. But I would like to go with your blessing.'

'And you have it.' He took her in his arms and stroked her hair, holding her tightly.

'Thank you, Father.'

* * *

Saying goodbye to Edgar was even more painful. He went with her to the station and hugged her tightly before she climbed aboard the train.

'Take care, my dear girl.'

As she sat in the compartment, she appreciated what a wonderful man he was. He had always treated her as if she were his own flesh and blood. There had never been any doubt in her mind that he loved her as much as her brothers.

15

Dear Father,

We arrived safely. Our hospital is made up of a series of tents within earshot of the fighting. The noise is a background to our lives. We work and live without many of the necessities, but are learning to make do. There is a feeling of friendship among us, and even the professional nurses are thawing and becoming our friends.

I am not able to tell you exactly where we are, but you are not to worry. Sometimes lines of soldiers march along the road near us, singing and heading for the front. It breaks my heart.

Your loving daughter,
Anna

Dear Anna,

I am pleased you got there safely and are working hard. All is well

here, much as usual.
Love,
Father
P.S. You know I am not a writer.

Dear Father,
The post gets here very quickly, which keeps up morale. It is a highlight of the day. I was happy to hear that life is going on as usual at home. Please let me know when you hear from my brothers.

We are kept busy scrubbing, bed-making, giving blanket baths and so on. The men are very grateful for what we do for them after being in the trenches, and many are cheerful and amuse one another.

I hope this letter finds you well.
Love,
Anna

Dear Anna,
We are busy with lambing and could do with you here. You were always good with the frail ones who

didn't feed from their dams.

I have had no word from Michael for several weeks. I worry for him. Robert and John tell me they are in good health, although they say little about the trenches.

Love,
Father

Dear Father,

It is wonderful to be in touch with you. I am not going to tell you all we have to deal with here in France. It is brutal and soul-destroying for the men. I often think of my brothers and pray they will survive the war. One of the tents is our church. We sing well-known hymns. We pray for the sick here and for those fighting. We have a piano and one of the patients usually plays. I remember Mother playing our piano at home.

I hope this letter finds you well.

Love,
Anna

Dear Anna,

I have some bad news. Michael has been injured. By the time you get this, he may be somewhere in England.

We are very busy on the farm as usual. It sounds as though you are kept busy too.

Love,
Father

Dear Father,

Please let me know as soon as you have more news of Michael. We are constantly caring for new casualties. Young men, like Michael, who face unimaginable horrors with strength and humour. After the trenches, it must be good to have hot food and a comfortable bed. We have a gramophone for entertainment and we play cards. Please keep writing, as it is a great comfort to hear from you.

Love,
Anna

My dear father, Henry,

You will be surprised to hear from me, but being so close to the war and seeing the casualties has made me think more about the living.

I thank you for those books you sent me after my mother's death. Although I had finished my schooling then, I persevered with my reading and writing and hope I am now able to write a reasonable letter. Perhaps you will reply and tell me.

With kindest wishes,
Anna

My dear Anna,

It was with great joy that I received your letter, which is very well written.

You will be interested to know the Hall is now a fully-fledged, and full, convalescent home. I have stayed in the country and involve myself as much as matron will allow! The men are mainly pragmatic and keep cheerful. We arrange entertainments to amuse them.

Sometimes I imagine you working here. I like to think of you as being safe. I try to keep up with my tenants' news. Jenkins has his sources, and in spite of his age, is still able to get around. As far as I know, your brothers are all still fighting. If only I was a younger man and could join them.

Your loving father,
Henry

My dear Henry,
Have you heard that Michael has been injured and returned to England? I think my mother would join me in begging you to do all in your power to get him moved to Wickwell Hall as soon as he is well enough. Father tells me he has shrapnel injuries.

I brought the mourning bracelet with me as a talisman. I keep it in my pocket and often feel it — the hard roundness of the beads and the cold metal of the locket. I often look at the drawings; it comforts me and makes me feel close to home.

Your loving daughter,
Anna

Dear Anna,
Michael is recovering well at
Wickwell Hall. I think the earl is
taking special care of him, for which I
am grateful.
I have more bad news. Your other
two brothers, John and Robert, are
both dead. I pray they were killed
instantly and suffered no pain.
Love,
Father

Dear Father,
How do you bear such loss? I feel
as though my heart is broken, and I
am exhausted from both the work
and grief.
How is Michael doing now? Please
give him my love when you next visit.
I fear he will soon be well enough to
return to the front.
Love,
Anna

My dear Henry,

I went for a short walk in the woods yesterday as I had a little time off. On the way, I passed a small patch of lily of the valley. I picked a stem and have pressed it as it reminded me of the engraving on the mourning locket. I still look at the drawings inside of my mother and you, my father.

As you know, Michael is being sent back to fight, but I thank you for the care you have given him over the past few months.

A small part of me is still shocked at the loss of life, but I am becoming used to it, which is perhaps most shocking of all.

Love,
Anna

Dear Anna,

Thank you for your last letter.

I have more sad news for you. The earl was out riding yesterday, and fell from his horse when it faltered at a

162

fence. *He broke his neck and his death would have been immediate.*

Love,
Father

Anna crumpled the letter and sobbed. He was dead. It was only recently, when she'd realised how short life was, that she'd decided to write to her father and include him in her life. The grief was all too much. The loss of life, the ruined lives. Henry wasn't a casualty of war, but he was her father and now he was dead.

The next day she received a letter from him.

My dear Anna,

I apologise for not replying to your most recent letter sooner. We have been very busy here and I wanted to write more than a hurried note. I think the war has made me realise how important loving relationships are.

I want you to know I loved your mother more than you can imagine.

But when she needed my support, I abandoned her. She was a strong woman and kind. She gave me the freedom to carry out my duty, which was to marry Elizabeth. We have both been miserable in the marriage, and Elizabeth's unfulfilled desire to have children has turned her into a bitter woman.

Happily, your mother had an agreeable life. She had a supportive husband, and children, more than she could have thought possible when she left the Hall. Your mother was a good woman and Edgar a good man. My loss was his gain.

I would like to get to know you better. Maybe after the war, when you are safely home again, we can see each other. It would bring me joy and, I hope, bring you pleasure.

Your letters do you merit. I am glad the books I sent you were of some help in your learning. It was little enough.

But, for now, goodbye until the next letter.

Your loving father,
Henry

There would be no next letter. After re-reading what he had written, tears flowing down her cheeks, Anna folded the letter and added it to all the other letters from home which she kept tied with a ribbon. She felt a need to look at the drawings in the mourning locket and reached into her pocket for it. She leapt up in panic when she couldn't find it. Throwing things about, she searched all her belongings, then sat on the camp bed and tried to think. When had she last had the locket? She remembered feeling it on the previous day's walk. But then scrabbling across some rocks over a little stream, she'd stumbled and fallen. It could be in the stream, washed away. She told herself it didn't matter. Who would find it and wonder at the drawings and the lock of downy baby hair? What would they add to the locket? Would they cherish it?

16

BARBARA AND DOREEN —
World War Two

Doreen put her hand in her pocket and let the chain trickle through her fingers until she felt the solidness of the locket. She imagined the coloured enamel lily of the valley leaves and the patterns decorating it, the picture of a church on the back, and then she thought of the sepia photographs inside. Barbara laughing and Pete serious in his uniform. The locket was a token of his love for her, but now her friend was dead.

A sob from the pew at the front of the church brought her back to her friend's funeral with a jolt. It was unbearable to think of Barbara lying in the solid wooden coffin on the bier before them.

A noise from along the pew made her turn to see Joe dabbing at his face with a handkerchief. He was wretched, and she wished there was some way she could comfort him. She couldn't help but pity him. It hadn't been his fault. It had been an unfortunate accident.

★ ★ ★

Two years previously, on the train journey from London, Doreen had become anxious. She worried that she'd miss her station. Signs had been removed to confuse the enemy.

When the train stopped at what she thought was her destination, a rural station in Norfolk, she almost immediately crossed to the other platform to get the next train back home. Instead, she took a deep breath and made her way out to the road, and after putting her canvas bag on the ground with her gas mask perched on top, waited.

A young woman of about her age joined her. 'Are you a Land Girl too?' she asked.

'Yes. I was told someone from Three

Trees Farm would pick me up from the train.'

'Me too. I'm Barbara, Barbara Booth. I've never stayed in the country before. It looks . . . empty.' She waved her arm around at the landscape. 'I'm a town girl. But I suppose this is an adventure and we have to do our bit for the war. Beat the enemy.' She ran a hand through her fair wavy hair. 'Mum says we'll get plenty to eat on a farm. She's sure there won't be any rationing. Maybe we'll get lots of butter and cream. Can't wait to get my curves back.' She giggled.

A car drove along the empty road towards them and stopped. A young man got out slowly and carefully, and nodded. 'Hello. Are you two for Three Trees Farm?'

'We are,' Barbara answered. 'Don't you have petrol rationing in the country?'

He smiled. 'Of course we do, but we've been saving our ration to pick you two up!'

As he slung their bags in the boot, Barbara nudged Doreen. 'Quite good-looking for a country boy, isn't he?'

'You're Barbara and Doreen?' Without waiting for an answer he continued, 'I'm Joe Thurston. My dad owns one of the farms where you'll be working. Looks like you've brought the sun with you.' He looked up at the sky, which was picture-book blue with cotton wool clouds.

The two young women sat together in the back of the Ford. Doreen felt at ease with the other young woman and was pleased to have met her. It would be nice to have someone to talk to and have as a friend.

'Where are you from?' Barbara asked.

'Willesden, north London. What about you?'

'We don't live too far from each other. I live in Hammersmith.'

Doreen thought they might live near each other, but they seemed a world apart, Barbara with her posh accent.

Barbara took a lipstick and compact

from her bag and touched up her make-up. 'I have to confess I don't know anything about farms or living in the country. I worked in an office, which was boring, and I wanted to do my bit for the war effort so decided to give it a go. I nearly gave up when I went for the training. How was yours?'

'We hardly learnt anything, but I suppose we'll learn as we go along.'

'I'm going to miss my mum and dad. I live with them and my four brothers,' Barbara chatted merrily. 'But now three of them are in the army and only the little one is still at home. Do you have brothers and sisters?'

'I have an older sister. Married with one child. She married her childhood sweetheart. I was working in a factory, but thought working on the land might be better.' The other reason she'd left was to erase thoughts of her ex-boyfriend. 'Have you got a boyfriend?' As she asked, she noticed Joe glancing at them in the mirror. He had nice eyes, a deep earth-brown.

'I have, so it's no good you thinking you'll be going out with me, Joe Thurston.' Barbara giggled again.

Doreen liked her cheekiness and wished she had the confidence to say things like that. 'So what's he like, this man of yours?'

'Pete? Tall, good-looking, kind. He's in the army. I miss him a lot. I'm terrified for him.'

As tears gathered in Barbara's eyes, Doreen reached over and squeezed her hand. 'I expect the war will be over soon. We'll all be back to normal before you know it.' She didn't believe it herself, so doubted Barbara would take any comfort from her words. 'Do you have a photo?'

Barbara reached into her bag and produced a crumpled sepia photograph. She smoothed it out. 'I look at him several times a day.'

As Doreen took the photo, she remembered her mum saying that beauty is in the eye of the beholder. Pete wasn't exactly good-looking in her eyes, but he had gentle features. He was wearing his uniform and had written in tiny writing across the bottom corner: *To my darling Barbara, all my love.* 'He looks nice.'

'He's lovely. We want to get married as soon as we can. What about you? Do you have a boyfriend?'

'No. I did, but when he got called up he met somebody in the ATS, and that was that. He sent me a letter telling me about her and how he hadn't really loved me after all. I don't care.'

Barbara nudged her, nodded in the direction of Joe, and then winked. They both laughed.

'Maybe,' Doreen whispered. 'He's not bad-looking.' Truthfully, she thought he was very attractive.

In the silence that followed, Joe said, 'The pigs will need mucking out when we get back.'

'Really?' Barbara asked. 'Don't we get time to settle into our new digs?'

Joe didn't reply, but grinned at them. Doreen looked out of the window. The countryside was pretty, with the trees in full leaf and wild flowers along the verges and hedgerows. It was a change from the greyness around her home. She could enjoy living in the country as long as the work wasn't too back-breaking. Barbara seemed as though she might be a good friend and fun to be with.

As they pulled into the farmyard, a middle-aged woman, followed by two dogs, appeared from the farmhouse and gave them a wave. 'That's Mum. She'll show you where you're staying. I've got work to do.' With that, Joe got out of the car and quickly hobbled away towards a large barn on the opposite side of the lane, hens scuttling out of his way. Doreen wondered why he limped.

'I'm Mrs Thurston. I'll take you to the Drews', where you are billeted. They're a caring, generous couple and she keeps a tidy house. Come with me.'

Mrs Thurston looked just how Doreen expected a farmer's wife to look, with her rosy cheeks, floral wrapover apron and rubber boots. The collies sniffed at Doreen's legs, so she quickly made a fuss of them, and then caught up with Mrs Thurston and Barbara.

'I hope you girls will like it here. You've been lucky getting a place at the Drews'. The other girls working on the local farms are all together in what we call the hostel, but there's no more room there. If you have any questions, I'm usually in the kitchen. Just knock and come in. If I'm not there, I won't be far off. And don't mind my husband, Mr Thurston. He's a bit gruff and has a lot to see to. But he has a good heart. Here's the church, it dates back a long way if you're interested in history. This is the oldest bit of the village. These cottages have been here a few hundred years.'

'Aren't they pretty with the roses and hollyhocks?' Doreen tried to imagine living in one of the cottages with their tiny windows and crooked walls. Most

174

of the cottages had diagonal patterns of brown sticky paper over the windows. But the gardens were unspoilt and full of flowers.

They passed the post office and village shop, and shortly afterwards Mrs Thurston opened a gate and led them up a path to another cottage. 'This is the Drews'.'

When they had knocked on the back door and let themselves into the kitchen, Doreen was pleased to see it was just as Mrs Thurston had promised: clean and tidy. The smell of baking reminded her that she was feeling hungry, and her stomach rumbled. She felt a hand squeeze hers, and she and Barbara smiled at each other. It seemed they were both pleased with the accommodation.

'Hello, hello. Sit yourselves down at the table and I'll make a cup of tea.' A woman bustled in and set about producing scones and cups of strong tea. At last she sat down with them. 'I'm Mrs Drew. Which one of you is which?' After they'd introduced themselves, Mrs Drew laid down a few rules. 'No coming in at all hours and no men folk here at the house. Keep your room spotless and neat. No loud noise. And I don't want any light showing when it's blackout. Mr Drew and I are very careful about that. We don't want any bombs dropping on us because of a chink of light. You stick to those rules and we'll get along very well.'

Doreen nodded as Barbara said, 'Certainly, Mrs Drew.'

'And I'll need your ration books.'

'Of course. We'll give them to you as soon as we unpack.'

'How's Mr Drew keeping?'

'Not too badly. He's at a meeting in the church hall. All the old men of the village are there discussing how to tackle the Germans if they land.' Both she and Mrs Thurston laughed. 'We know it's serious, girls, but you haven't seen them. It's a good job we've got Joe in the local civil defence or we'd be lost.'

'But why is Joe still here in the village? Hasn't he been called up?' Barbara asked.

Mrs Thurston looked down at her hands. 'They don't want him. He had an accident when he was eleven. He and his friends decided they'd scythe the grass along the lane. They knew they shouldn't be doing it. Poor Joe cut his leg so badly it had to be amputated below the knee.' She looked up and took a deep breath. 'That's why he limps and can't join the army. It knocked his confidence to start with, but he was determined it wouldn't stop him doing anything. But seeing all his friends going off to fight hasn't done him any good. He doesn't want sympathy, though. He wants to be treated like any other young man.' There was an awkward silence.

'But we're very happy to have him in the village,' Mrs Drew said. 'We need some young people brightening us up, especially with all the bombs being dropped. How much longer? That's what I want to know.'

After Mrs Thurston had left, Doreen and Barbara were led upstairs and shown their room. It was small and the two beds took up almost all the space. 'I'll leave you to make yourselves at home,' Mrs Drew said.

Barbara threw her bag on the floor and stretched out on the patchwork quilt on her bed. 'I wonder what the entertainment is round here.'

'I expect it's having singsongs and going to the pub. Anyway, I expect we'll be too exhausted for going out. Once we start picking potatoes or whatever they do at this time of year. I don't know anything about farming. I'm going to unpack, write a letter to my mum and dad, and then it will be about time for tea I should think.'

'Good idea. I'm going to unpack too, then I'll write to Pete. We're managing to keep in touch quite well.' She waved the photo of Pete. 'Here, have a better look. He's quite handsome, isn't he?'

Doreen took the photo again and looked at the smart uniformed soldier.

She wished she could say she had a boyfriend to write to and felt a pang of jealousy. Joe hadn't said much, but he'd seemed nice enough and she liked him. It sounded as though there wouldn't be any other young men on the farm or in the village. 'Tell me about him.'

'I've known him almost all my life. He lives in the next road so I saw a lot of him when I was growing up. When I was sixteen he asked me to go to the pictures. You can imagine how much my brothers pulled my leg about that.'

'Not really. I've only got a sister.'

'Lucky you. I'd have liked a sister. I'm right in the middle of my four brothers.' She made a face. 'I went out with Pete and that was that.'

'You fell in love?'

'We did. As I said, we want to get married as soon as this wretched war is over. He's in training, but can't tell me much with the letters being censored. He's a sergeant in the paras. Only twenty-five, but it's not like in peacetime when you'd be ancient before you were promoted.' Barbara sighed. 'I try not to think of where he's going to be sent and what's going on.' Barbara wriggled into a sitting position. 'What about you? We'll have to find you a boyfriend. I'm sure there must be a few local men left hiding away somewhere who aren't old enough to be your grandad. Do you think there'll be things to do? Like dances?'

'I don't know. Mrs Drew and Mrs Thurston were talking about the American base just down the road before Mrs Thurston left. Maybe they'll have entertainment and invite us.' Doreen pulled her uniform out of her bag. 'What do you think of this? Fancy having to wear breeches.'

'They are to give us the same freedom of movement as men have.'

'What about the hat?' Doreen put it on askew and was pleased she made Barbara giggle.

'Now *that* I could do without!'

17

Doreen and Barbara soon got to know the Thurston family and the other Land Girls working on the farms. On their first very early morning, Joe had taken them to one side and said, 'Before you start work, I want to show you something.' He led them into a barn and proudly gestured at the green tractor in front of them. 'What do you think of that? It's a David Brown. She's a beauty, isn't she?'

'She certainly is, Joe,' Barbara answered, a twinkle in her voice and eye. 'I expect you take your dates out on it.'

Doreen giggled.

Joe was silent for a moment, then laughed; a deep rumble. 'Not all farms have a tractor, you know. We're very modern.'

'We'll have to immobilise it if the enemy ever get near. That's what we were told in our training, anyway. Not that the enemy stands a chance. Especially not with Mr Drew and his pals on guard. What else have you got? Give us a tour before we start work,' Barbara said.

'I'll quickly show you the animals. We've got horses which still do some of the work on the farm, as well as pigs, cows and chickens. You'll probably get to know them all well because you'll be mucking out and all sorts. But first you need to get on with the milking.'

'Ooh, I thought we were just going to have an easy time collecting eggs in a basket and lying about in the hay staring up at the sky with straw stuck in our mouths.'

'I can see I'm going to have trouble with you, Barbara Booth. Now come on, I'll show you how to milk a cow.'

'I thought you said you were modern. Haven't you heard of milking machines?'

'That's the next thing we want, but meantime it's hard graft.'

As they walked back to their billet at

the end of their first day, they were both exhausted. Barbara rubbed her arms. 'Every muscle in my body aches. We've been working for hours. It's slave labour. They could have started us off more easily.'

'We *were* warned the days would be long. Oh, look, they must be some of the village women.' A group of four women were walking along the road, but stopped to stare at the two Land Girls.

'They should go back where they came from. We don't want them here with their breeches and fast ways,' one of the women said loudly to the others.

Barbara stopped too and Doreen tugged at her arm. 'Come on, Barbara, ignore them. We were told the local women might be hostile.'

'Well, it's not fair. We're doing our bit for the war effort. We all know there won't be enough food if we don't produce it ourselves.'

'I expect they're doing their bit too. Let's get back to the Drews'. They've been welcoming and accepted us.'

Sitting at the scrubbed wooden table with Mr and Mrs Drew to eat a meal of stew and potatoes, the young women tucked in.

'We can tell you've both worked hard today. You've got the appetite of heavy horses!'

'They're lovely, aren't they, Mr Drew?' Doreen said.

'Wonderful animals. It's a pity the tractors are taking over. Joe Thurston is as proud of that tractor they've got as if it was the crown jewels. He's a nice lad, that Joe. One of you two might suit him.'

'Don't make us blush,' Barbara said. 'We heard there are Americans down the road. Now they might be worth befriending with their nylons and chocolate.'

'You steer well clear of them; they're nothing but trouble to our village girls.' Mrs Drew was grim-faced. 'Nice girls like you couldn't do better than a local lad. Look at my Mr Drew.'

Barbara and Doreen both looked at Mr Drew with his blood-vessel cheeks, sparse hair and pot belly. 'Are you both from the village?' Barbara asked.

'Mr Drew is, and I'm from the next village. We met at chapel. We've been married forty-five years and are still going strong. Those Americans will love you and leave you.'

'They might not want to though, might they? I mean leave you. They go up in the planes and don't come back. It's not their choice.' Barbara put her knife and fork together on her empty plate.

'You're right, Barbara, love. They're brave young men.'

They sat in silence for a while before Mrs Drew said, 'Now I've got apple crumble and custard for anyone who's still hungry.'

'I can scarcely keep my eyes open, but I'd like a small bit, please. Then I'd like to go to bed. We have an early start again and I feel as though I've been run over by a steam engine.' Doreen ate the pudding quickly and was soon in bed. She heard the light switch click.

'Are you all right, Doreen?'

'I think so. I feel exhausted. I'm not sure how I'll manage tomorrow. I never imagined this.'

'I feel just the same. But we'll get used to it. We must remember why we're here and think of all the men who are fighting. We've got it easy compared to them.'

'I know you're right. I'm sure we'll feel better in the morning.'

⋆　⋆　⋆

Doreen felt as though she'd only just closed her eyes when Barbara shook her awake very early the following morning.

They dressed in silence and were soon back at the scrubbed wooden table eating large bowls of porridge.

'And how are you feeling today?' Mrs Drew poured tea for them.

'Aching all over. As though another

day of physical work will be torture. I expect we'll have the milking to start off with. It's far too early. I'm sure even the cows don't like their early starts. Joe said he'd take me on his milk round afterwards, so I might get out of the field work for a bit,' said Barbara.

Doreen immediately felt jealous. Why had Joe asked Barbara, not her? She tried to suppress her feelings and remembered the wink one of the Italian prisoners of war had given her the previous day. He was a good-looking dark-haired young man. She'd never met the enemy before and hadn't known how to react, so had turned away. 'I suppose we have to think of the POWs as the enemy. Some of the other girls seemed quite friendly with them. It's very confusing.'

Mrs Drew sat at the table and sipped her tea. 'They're the same as our young men. They were sent to fight. It wasn't their choice. They are someone's son, brother, father, husband. Treat them like you would a local.'

'Talking of locals, we weren't made to feel welcome by some of the village women yesterday. We were told to go back where we came from, with our breeches and fast ways,' Barbara said.

'Oh, dear, oh dear. That will be Mrs Wright and her friends. When they get to know you, those women will change their minds about you. Ignore them. It's their fear of the unknown, I suppose. A bit like you and the prisoners, Doreen.'

★　★　★

A few weeks later, they were in a field, clearing it of thistles and other weeds. The air was damp and mist hung about the hedges and in the ditches, which they knew would soon be burnt off by the sun. Doreen's back ached. It seemed to hurt continuously. The days were long, and in the evenings she craved her bed. The only things that kept her going were the companionship, seeing Joe, and the thought that she was helping in the war. Doreen had learnt to like leaning in against the cows and feeling their steamy heat as the milk streamed into the bucket. It had been exhausting at first, but as her muscles had got used to the exercise she had started to enjoy it, although the early mornings were hard. And once the cows had been milked, she and the other girls were sent out to work in the fields. Her favourite times were when she was with the animals. She particularly liked leading the horses when they were out working. She'd been especially pleased that morning when Joe had praised her.

'You've a way with animals, Doreen. None of the other Land Girls manage what you do with them.'

That was all, but it was enough to keep her smiling the whole day.

'Fancy the pictures tonight, Doreen?' Barbara asked.

'I'm not sure. I feel too tired to do anything.'

'Joe's said he'll take us.'

'Has he? I might come. I'll see.'

'He says we can leave work early,' Barbara added.

Doreen was already wondering how to style her hair and whether she should wear the nylons an American serviceman, Bud, had sent her after they'd met at a recent dance. When the packet had been delivered, she'd tried to hide it so that Mrs Drew wouldn't see. But Barbara had grabbed it and asked, 'Who's it from? Secret admirer. Come on, let's see what's in it.'

She'd had to open it in the kitchen and Mrs Drew had tutted her disapproval. Going out with Joe would be an excuse to wear the stockings. It would be good to feel feminine. If only it was just her and Joe going.

*   *   *

They didn't hear the engine of the car, so were surprised when Joe knocked on the back door and walked into the kitchen before they'd finished their meal and had time to change.

190

'Sorry, ladies, the Ford's broken. We can cycle, but we need to get going if we want to get there on time.'

'We haven't got bikes, Joe,' Barbara told him. 'It's a good job we didn't have time to dress up. Doreen wouldn't have wanted to ladder her new nylons. She's got an admirer — one of the Americans.'

Doreen wished Barbara had kept quiet about Bud and his present.

'The Chapmans at the post office have agreed to lend you their bicycles. It's only a few minutes' walk to their cottage,' said Joe.

It wasn't quite how Doreen had imagined the outing. She and Barbara were still in their breeches and their hair was a mess. But Barbara didn't seem to mind. She chatted easily as they cycled along the narrow country roads, and Joe laughed a lot with her. Doreen's bike was heavy, and with her body aching, she could barely keep up.

'Come on, slowcoach,' Joe called back.

She didn't even get to sit next to Joe at the picture house. Barbara sat between them and frequently whispered in Joe's ear. Doreen couldn't understand why she was flirting with another man when she had said she was in love with Pete. And it was clear to her that Joe preferred Barbara to any of the other girls on the farm.

After the film, Barbara said she wanted to go to one of the pubs in the town.

'I'm not going into a pub dressed like this,' Doreen said.

'Aren't you the proper one,' Barbara mocked.

But surprisingly, Joe stuck up for her. 'I think Doreen's right. We've got a long ride back and you've got another hard day tomorrow. We'll come out again another evening. Race you to the bend.'

Barbara hopped on her bike and hurtled after him while Doreen took her time setting off. She followed them, and as she tried to squeeze past the pair on the narrow road, she skidded and sped off into a ditch. She could hear Barbara laughing as Joe bounded into the ditch and helped pull her out.

'Are you all right? Definitely no bones broken. Hang on, your arm is covered in blood. You must have grazed it on something. Right, we'll leave the bikes here and walk back. It's not far now. I'll collect the bikes in the morning. Barbara, you can ride back. I'll look after Doreen.'

Barbara looked disappointed. 'I'm sorry I laughed. It was really funny the way you flew into the ditch. I'm sorry you're hurt. Can't I walk back too?'

'There's no point, and you'll be expected to work first thing in the morning. Doreen, take my arm with your good one.'

Although her grazed arm hurt, Doreen enjoyed being taken care of by Joe and having him to herself once Barbara had left with a sulky look on her face.

'Are you okay?' he asked. 'Not feeling faint?'

'I haven't lost that much blood!'

'I meant from the shock. You'll have to have some strong sweet tea and maybe a drop of Mum's wine or sloe gin.'

When they arrived back at the farmhouse, no one was in the kitchen. 'Mum and Dad go to bed early. You sit here and I'll get a cloth to clean your arm, and then we'll dab some antiseptic on.'

Joe very tenderly wiped her arm with a clean, damp cloth, holding her hand as he did so. 'Now this next bit may sting.'

Doreen winced as he patted her graze with the liquid.

'Are you comfortable? I'll fetch some cushions for you to lean on and then I'll make tea.'

Doreen watched as he busied himself round the kitchen. He was tall and muscular. She supposed all the physical work he did on the farm made him strong.

After the tea and a glass of parsnip wine, Joe took her hand again and leaned over, inspecting her injury. He was so close, she couldn't resist. Her head spun as she lifted her face to his, gently pressing her mouth to his lips. Joe jumped out of his chair, almost falling as he struggled upright. He stood looking at her. 'What are you doing?' he shouted.

'I'm sorry, Joe. I'll go now. Thank you for looking after me,' she gabbled in her embarrassment. Her face felt hot.

'No, wait.'

Doreen's heart lifted. He did want to kiss her.

'Let's get this straight. I think you are a nice girl, but I don't want your sympathy.'

'Oh, but it wasn't like that.' She could feel tears welling.

'Why would anyone kiss someone like me? Because you feel sorry for me.' He stayed quiet for a moment, breathing hard and frowning. 'I won't say anything to anyone about this, if you keep it to yourself too.'

'Don't worry, Joe, I won't tell anyone what a fool I've made of myself.'

'I'll walk you home. You can come in to work later tomorrow. I'll explain to Dad.'

They walked to the Drews' in silence and wished each other a curt goodnight on parting. Doreen asked herself why she had been so forward. She hadn't been able to help herself. Why had she thought it was the right thing to do? With the questions unanswered, she quietly sobbed herself to sleep.

★   ★   ★

The next morning, Doreen had time to reflect on the situation. She thought she'd fallen in love with Joe, but he'd made it quite clear he wasn't interested in her. Maybe she should accept the request for a date from Bud. She liked him, but there wasn't that same feeling in the pit of her stomach she felt when Joe was about. She found Mrs Drew in the kitchen.

'How are you doing, love?'

'All right, thank you.'

196

'There's some porridge in the pot on the stove if you fancy it. Our Barbara wasn't in the best of moods this morning. Something's got under her skin.'

'I expect she'll be all right. Maybe she's missing home. I was wondering if you'd like these.' She held the stockings out and Mrs Drew took them from her.

'Lovely — I won't say no if you're sure. But aren't you going to be seeing Bud? He's sent you a few notes as well as the gift.'

'I might. I'm not sure. I expect he thinks I'm not interested as I haven't said I'll go out with him. I expect he's already found someone else. Plenty of the girls like the Americans with their chocolate and sweets.'

'No doubt.' Her tone was disapproving, but Doreen was amused she hadn't baulked at accepting Bud's nylons. 'Joe will miss you next week. You're being sent to the Warbys' farm. They've a lot of work that needs doing.'

Doreen's first thought was that this

move was something to do with Joe. He didn't want her around. But then she realised he wasn't in a position to make such a major decision. She also realised that he and Barbara wouldn't be very happy at being separated. It was then that Doreen realised why he hadn't wanted to kiss her. Barbara had taken his heart. Barbara, who already had a boyfriend she planned to marry. It wasn't easy to accept that the man she had fallen in love with was in love with her unobtainable best friend.

18

It wasn't long before Bud turned up at the Drews' cottage, a bunch of wild flowers in his arms. Doreen and Barbara were sitting at the kitchen table mending their clothes, having made friends again after the bicycle incident. Mrs Drew invited him to join them and offered to make him a cup of tea.

'Well, thanks. Your tea is what keeps us Yanks, as you call us, going. It's going to help us win the war. I hope you don't mind me stopping by. I've brought Doreen some flowers.' He handed over the bunch and sat down at the table.

'They're lovely, Bud, thank you.' Doreen held them to her nose to inhale their sweet smell.

''Fraid I couldn't buy some. These are what your English countryside provided. I was wondering if you young women want to come to the dance tomorrow. We'll send a jeep to collect you.'

'Oh, I don't know.' Doreen wasn't sure she wanted to get involved with him. She liked him, but he was too keen. Maybe he had to be. The clock was ticking for him. If you counted every plane setting off, you could be almost certain there would be fewer to count when they came back. It made her want to cry. Those poor young men, their families. How were they all going to bear the terrible tragedy of this war? It wouldn't be kind to turn him down. 'Yes, we'll come, won't we, Barbara? Thank you, Bud.'

'Swell.' He gulped down his tea and stood to leave. Then he reached into his pocket and pulled out a bar of chocolate. 'For you, ma'am,' he said as he handed it to Mrs Drew.

'Thank you, but you don't get round me that easily. I want my girls back at a reasonable time. They have to be up at the crack of dawn.'

'I know, and I'll see them safely home

before midnight. I'll look after them, ma'am.' With that, he made his way out.

Mrs Drew harrumphed, but Doreen noticed her tucking the chocolate into the pocket of her apron.

★　★　★

The two young women helped each other with their make-up and hair. They had brought very little with them in the way of non-working clothes, but they both had flared skirts and pretty poplin blouses. When they heard the knock on the back door, they ran down the stairs.

Doreen enjoyed dancing with Bud. He knew the moves, and soon they were swinging, swaying, reeling and spinning. She quickly picked up some of the new steps. When they were hot and tired, he went to get refreshments. Doreen looked round for Barbara and gave her a little wave. She was surrounded by men and looked to be enjoying the attention.

'Here you are, soda.' Bud handed her a glass.

'Thanks, I'm thirsty.' She gulped at the fizzy drink. 'That was fun. I love dancing.'

'Me too,' he said.

She realised they knew nothing about each other. This was just a moment in time they were sharing and they would probably never know each other very well. She felt a shadow fall over the hall.

'Hey, what's up? Come on, it's the lindy hop. We have to dance this one.' Bud took the glass and put it down on a table then grabbed her hand and led her on to the dance floor again.

In bed that night, Doreen thought back on the evening. It had almost felt frenzied. The need to dance, to enjoy yourself. But she liked Bud and hoped to see him again. She didn't think she'd ever be *in* love with him, but he was kind and good fun. If he survived the war, he'd go back home to America. They might as well enjoy being with each other, whatever happened. Tears welled in her eyes as she prayed Bud and his fellow servicemen would be safe.

* * *

The weeks turned into months, and they got used to the routine of working on the land. Doreen and Joe acted just as they had before her attempt to kiss him. Barbara and Joe still messed about together, and it was clear from his behaviour that she'd been right, Joe was in love with Barbara.

Doreen kept her thoughts to herself. She too enjoyed Barbara's company. She was a funny, lively young woman with an overwhelming zest for life. And she was kind. When the prisoners of war picked flowers from the meadows and offered them, she always accepted graciously, whereas a few of the other girls immediately slung them down on the ground. Barbara had also befriended the local women who had initially shunned them.

'Beautiful flowers in the church last Sunday, Mrs Wright,' Barbara said when they met the women walking through the village one day.

Doreen was surprised she'd seen the flowers, because as far as she knew, Barbara had worked Sunday morning then spent most of the afternoon lying in bed recovering from the previous week of hard farm work.

Mrs Wright looked surprised, but replied stiffly, 'Thank you.'

'You should do classes. Teach us town girls how to do arrangements.'

Doreen could see the woman was beginning to warm to Barbara. 'That's an idea. When could we have them?'

'We're occasionally free Saturday afternoon and sometimes on Sunday, but you wouldn't want to do it on Sunday.'

'Saturdays I go to Diss to spend the day with my old mum. That's a pity.'

'It is, Mrs Wright. It's a pity too we have to work such long hours.'

'You do work hard. All in a good cause.'

'Feeding the nation. We need to get on with it. See you soon.' And with that, Barbara gave a warm smile and the two girls carried on.

'You're good with people, but did you see the flowers in church?' Doreen asked.

'I found out from Mrs Drew what Mrs Wright does round the village, and she said the church flowers were her responsibility. I didn't want to lie, so I popped into the church on Sunday after we'd eaten. They really were very good. I'd also found out she wasn't available on Saturday afternoons, just in case she was prepared to do classes then.'

'I really thought you were keen.'

'I'd rather pick potatoes than arrange flowers. But I think Mrs Wright and her friends might be nicer to us now.'

And they were. All the young women incomers noticed a difference in the attitude of the previously hostile women and even received small gifts of freshly baked bread or jam occasionally.

★   ★   ★

It was strange how at home she felt in the country, Doreen reflected as she and Barbara walked to work one winter morning. The work was harder than she'd ever imagined, and being outside all day whatever the weather was challenging and demanding. She tried to picture living in the village permanently in peacetime. Would she like it once the other girls had gone home? She thought she would, then she reminded herself that once they'd won the war, she would be going home too.

Then she thought of Joe. She couldn't imagine never seeing him again. And Bud? Everyone thought she was serious about him, but her feelings weren't any stronger than when she'd first met him. What she liked best was dancing with him. It was exhilarating moving to the music and being completely in tune with each other.

And then the inevitable happened. Bud's friend, Chuck, turned up. He removed his cap and twisted it in his hands.

'I'm sorry to bring you bad news, Doreen. We lost two planes today.' His voice wavered. 'Bud was in one of them. I'm sorry.' He quickly left the cottage and they saw him moments later, leaning against the shed, his body shaking. Doreen watched him, scarcely able to believe what she'd just been told. They'd been dancing only two nights previously. Bud had been alive and happy.

'Drink this, my girl.' Mrs Drew placed a glass of elderberry wine in front of her. 'We'll have one too. Fetch two more glasses, Barbara.'

Mr Drew marched into the room. 'They've dug up the village cricket pitch! No one told me they were going to do that. It's an outrage.' He stopped shouting and looked at the three women. 'What's happened?'

'It's Bud, Doreen's young man. He's dead. He may have been American, but he wasn't like the others. I liked him.' Mrs Drew wiped her face with her apron. 'It's all right to cry, Doreen. No need to be brave. We're your family.'

With that, Doreen burst into tears.

She didn't cry for herself, but for Bud, the life he'd never have, and his family.

Once she'd calmed down, the others started talking about everyday things as though it would take their lives back to normal. Normal? Doreen couldn't imagine normal. Normal wasn't young men dropping bombs on civilians and being killed in the process.

'We did it, Mr Drew,' Barbara said.

'Did what, Barbara?'

'We ploughed up the cricket pitch. Under orders, of course. Doreen worked the hardest. We were using the horses as the tractor was up in the top field. The pitch is going to be worked to grow food. You can't complain about that.'

'Where is the village going to play cricket in the summer? That's what I want to know.' Mr Drew reached for Mrs Drew's glass and took a swig of wine.

Mrs Drew sighed. 'Who is there left to play cricket? Joe and a few others doing essential war work. Let's wait until after the war to think about village cricket.'

Doreen closed her eyes and pictured Bud looking into her eyes and laughing as they'd held each other and danced together. They'd lived for the moment, and now the moment was gone.

★   ★   ★

On the farm the following day, after she and Barbara had finished milking, Joe said, 'Barbara, will you take the cows back to the barn? We'll keep them inside while it's still wet, cold and windy.' He took Doreen's arm, leading her to a corner of the milking shed. 'I'm very sorry. About Bud. I didn't know him, but Barbara said you and he were fond of each other and he often brought you gifts. She told me how much you enjoyed dancing and being together.'

'Thanks, Joe. I'm very sad for him, his family and his friends. It's such a waste.' Tears welled, and Joe took her in his arms and held her tightly.

'If you want time off, I'm sure it will be all right,' he said.

She sniffed and pulled away. 'No, I'm all right. Better to keep busy.'

He stroked her hair away from her face. 'I wish I could join up. I'm a fraud. I can do everything and yet I'm not allowed to fight for my country.' He smiled. 'There is something I haven't mastered though, and that's dancing. I trip over myself.'

Doreen smiled back, knowing he was trying to cheer her up. 'You'll have to get Barbara to teach you. If you start with something slow, you'll learn. Ask her.'

Joe put his hands in his pockets. 'Well, if you're sure you're okay, I think we'd better get to work.'

★　★　★

Pete was exhausted. The challenge of the past months had kept him going, but having achieved their objective by battling through France and reaching

Berlin, he'd begun to relax and now he felt drained. The things he'd done and sights he'd seen were almost too much to bear. But they'd won. Peace was in their grasp.

He lay on a makeshift bed in the bombed-out hotel they'd requisitioned. He imagined the small hotel had once been quite smart, but now the windows had been blown out, some of the walls were destroyed and the plumbing and electrics were wrecked. When he tried to sleep, scenes from the past came back to him like scenes in a story. The training in England had been tough, but landing behind enemy lines in France the previous June had been the worst day of his life up to that point. Half the men who parachuted in with him had died. Mistakes had been made, and men he'd become close to had simply landed in the marshes and sunk. But those men who had landed safely had a mission, and the following months were spent fighting their way through France and Germany, blowing up bridges and Nazi communication posts as they went. Some things he would never talk about.

Pete had known they'd won the war in Europe when they'd arrived in Berlin. Meeting Russian soldiers, they'd shaken hands and tried to communicate their pleasure at having beaten the enemy together. Surely there would be everlasting peace, he had thought.

And what now? Pete asked himself. The Germans had been beaten, but the previous day when out in the streets, he'd seen two small girls hiding in a house destroyed by the bombing. They'd looked scared and hungry. An elderly man appeared from another ruin and held something out to him. It was a locket. The man mimed smoking. Cigarettes for the locket? He reached into his pocket and took out a full packet and held them out to the man. They were snatched, and the locket was dropped into his hand. The man shuffled away. Pete took a closer look at the locket. It was gold with an enamelled decoration. Was it a family heirloom? Should he take it? He knew some soldiers were taking anything they could get their hands on, the spoils of war.

He spent the evening cleaning the locket and the chain it was on, as well as cutting photos of himself and Barbara to fit. He wrote a letter and put it in an envelope with the locket to send to her. After months of not being able to communicate with her, they'd started writing again, and she'd expressed her delight that he was safe and well and at last the war was coming to an end.

Little did she know about the dangers still facing the allied soldiers. He wouldn't tell her about the last pocket of Nazi resistance, the guerrillas who were killing their enemy at any opportunity.

19

Doreen looked out of the window as she sipped a glass of water. Bunting they'd put out to celebrate the end of the war still flapped idly in the breeze. The street party had been joyous, and Doreen had felt very much part of the village. She hadn't been well that morning and Mrs Drew had insisted she stay at home. The elderly postman walked up the path while Mrs Drew was out in the garden, and Doreen met him at the door.

'Parcel for Miss Booth.' He handed over the small package.

It was from Pete. Doreen placed it on the table and sat looking at it. She picked the package up and squeezed it. Whatever was in there wasn't very big. She couldn't wait for Barbara to open it.

When Barbara came back late that

evening, she was full of talk about her day.

'Joe's such a laugh. He had us all singing Italian songs. Even the POWs joined in. They're all very happy at the thought of going home soon.'

'We'll be going too, won't we?'

'Maybe not just yet. Joe says some of us will be needed to stay on and keep things going. Not all the men will be coming back and it will be a while before some of the injured ones are fit for work.'

'Do you want to stay?'

'Yes, I'm happy here. It's hard work, but we have a right laugh, don't we? What about you?'

'I'd like to stay too. But Pete will be coming home, won't he? You'll go home then?'

'In his last letter it didn't sound as though he knew when he'd be back. It might be ages before he can leave Germany. I'm going to make the most of being here.'

Of course you are, thought Doreen.

You're going to continue breaking Joe's heart. She regarded Barbara as her best friend, but that didn't mean she couldn't see her faults.

'I've just remembered. There's a parcel for you upstairs on your bed,' Doreen said.

Barbara took the stairs two at a time, calling back, 'Why didn't you tell me before?'

Doreen followed her, curious to know what Pete had sent. Barbara had already ripped open the package and held out its contents. It was a pretty locket. Golden with coloured leaves and patterns. On the back was a delicate engraving of a church. Barbara carefully opened the locket. Inside were pictures of Pete and Barbara. She picked up the letter and held it out for them both to read.

My dearest Barbara,
I bought this for you. We may not be together, but in the locket we are as close as we'll ever be. I can't say

216

much, but I hope to be home soon.
This peace will be everlasting. I can't
wait to marry you. I love you more
than words can say,
    Pete

'I want to wear this forever, so I can feel Pete close to me, but I can't risk losing it. I'll put it under my pillow when I'm at work.' Barbara clasped the locket tightly.

★   ★   ★

The following day was spent in some of the Thurstons' fields repairing fencing. It had rained most of the day and the ground was slippery with mud. At the end of the afternoon all the workers picked up their tools and started trudging back to the farm. Joe drove the tractor, which he'd used to transport the fence posts, and before they'd gone very far Barbara ran to catch up and begged for a lift.

'Joe, give this poor tired girl a ride.'

'It's not fair on the others, Barbara. It would be favouritism.'

'I *am* your favourite.' Barbara laughed.

'Jump up then,' Joe said, after stopping. They set off down the sloping field and started singing *It's a Long Way to Tipperary*. Barbara turned and waved at the rest of them trailing behind. Joe did the same and as he did so the tractor veered off into a shallow ditch and tipped over sideways. A terrible scream tore through the air before silence descended. Everyone ran to the upturned tractor. Joe clambered down and unsteadily walked round to the other side. It was obvious to them all that the tractor had crushed the life out of Barbara. He fell to his knees and sobbed.

Doreen felt a comforting arm around her from one of the other girls, and she too burst into tears.

Joe was muttering to himself, 'I killed her. I killed her.'

Doreen couldn't speak. She couldn't console Joe.

* ★ ★

Nothing felt the same after Barbara's death.

Mrs Drew's eyes were bloodshot, but she couldn't seem to stop talking. Maybe it saved her from thinking too much. 'The vicar told me Barbara's parents have decided she should be buried here. They said her letters were full of happiness, and they think she'd have liked being laid to rest in the village churchyard. We'll have the funeral tea here. Everyone will rally round. There might still be rationing, but we'll do her family proud.' Mrs Drew wiped her eyes with her apron. 'She was a lovely girl. I'd be happy to call you two girls my daughters. And poor Joe. No one's seen him since the accident. He's shut himself up. His mother says he's inconsolable.'

'I've heard other people in the village talking about how he's taken her death. Poor Joe,' Doreen said.

'You might be able to help him. He's

fond of you. Why don't you go round?'

'I don't think I'd do him any good.'

'Mr Drew and I think you should try. Barbara was your friend and so is he. But he needs you now.'

Doreen walked slowly through the village. She took a deep breath as she went through the open back door of the farmhouse into the kitchen. Unusually, there was no smell of cooking.

Mrs Thurston was sitting at the wooden table, her hands in her lap. 'Doreen. How are you?'

'All right. I came to see Joe.'

'I'm worried about him. He's hardly eating and not talking. No one else blames him, but he blames himself for Barbara's death. Tractor accidents happen all the time. It's one of those things. So much death. All those men killed in the war and now this. It breaks your heart.'

'Will you call him down?'

'He won't come. You go up. It's the room on the right of the landing.'

'Are you sure that's all right? I mean to go to his room.'

'Go, love.'

Doreen lifted the latch of the door at the bottom of the stairs and went up. As she climbed the stairs, she wondered what she could say. She knocked on his door. 'It's me, Doreen. I want to talk to you.' Without waiting for a reply, she opened the door and walked in. Joe was lying on the bed. He looked pale and had dark patches under his eyes.

Doreen sat on the edge of the bed. 'Joe, you mustn't blame yourself. I know you loved Barbara, but it wasn't your fault she died.'

'I wasn't paying attention. I should have thought about the mud and how easily the tractor would slide in it, especially on that slope. I was messing about.'

'And so was Barbara. She was encouraging you. That's what she was like. She liked a good time.'

'What about her family? And Pete? What about him? He wanted to marry her and now their future together is gone. Tell me how he's going to deal with that.' His voice rose and he sat up. 'I felt very close to her. She was . . . oh, I don't know . . . one bright star in a dark sky, but I always knew she'd leave to marry Pete.'

'I know what you mean, Joe.'

'She was always talking about you. Even when you'd had an argument, she'd tell me how happy she was you'd made up, how she wouldn't have managed being here without you. She loved you and she loved me, but she loved Pete too. What will he do?'

'In his last letter, he said he didn't know when he'd get back. Do you think he'll come to her funeral?'

'I don't know. I expect it's difficult.' Joe looked at her. 'Pete and your Bud have fought bravely. I feel so useless with my disability. I couldn't fight for my country like them.'

'You've kept the farm going to provide necessary food. You shouldn't feel ashamed.'

He reached out and took her hand. 'I should have joined up somehow. I would rather have died fighting than be responsible for killing Barbara.'

'There was no way you could have joined up. People have hidden their ages and all sorts in order to fight, but it was impossible for you. Anyway, your work here has been invaluable.' She squeezed his hand. In spite of the awful situation, holding hands with Joe somehow made her feel calmer.

'You're right, Doreen. There was no way I could hide my disability.'

Doreen had never seen him without his false leg and it shook her. Not seeing the physical absence, but thinking of all the problems he'd faced since he'd had the accident. 'There will be a lot more people coming back in your position or worse. Let's hope they face up to their difficulties as well as you have.'

'Maybe it's easier to adapt when you're young. I can live without my leg, but I can't deal with killing Barbara.'

'You must stop saying that. No one else thinks of it as anything other than a tragic accident. No one, no one at all, blames you. All I've heard is people being sympathetic and saying how sorry they are you've taken her death so badly and are blaming yourself.' Doreen knew there would always be a blank in their lives that was Barbara-shaped. 'Now promise me you'll go down and have something to eat when I've gone. Your mum is miserable worrying about you.'

'I promise.'

★　★　★

Doreen stood for the next hymn. She'd desperately hoped Pete would have been able to get back to England for Barbara's funeral. He'd written to her, and she'd read the letter so many times she could recite it word for word in her head.

> *Dear Doreen,*
> *Barbara told me a bit about you in the few letters I received from her. She said you were her dearest friend*

and she wouldn't have managed her time in the country without you. I thank you for that. We have lost the loveliest, sweetest woman. Often when I was in the depths of despair over the situation we found ourselves in, both in France and Germany, I told myself a peaceful life with Barbara would make everything worthwhile.

I will not be able to get back for her funeral. Please write and tell me every detail. And I have another favour to ask you. Will you look through her things and make sure she received a pretty locket on a chain with photos of her and me inside? It will be a great comfort to me to know she received a token of my affection, and that she read the accompanying letter in which I told her my feelings for her.

Say goodbye to my darling Barbara for me.

Kindest regards,
Pete

* ★ ★ ★

As they left the church and went into the churchyard, it was raining heavily. Hats were put on and umbrellas opened. Mrs Wright walked over to Doreen. 'How are you bearing up, love?' She put her umbrella over both of them.

'All right.'

'It's the worst thing, losing a dear friend or relative. Most of us know that now.'

'Yes, it seems that everyone has lost someone during the past few years. I can't thank you enough for doing the flower arrangements for the church. Those pretty flowers would have pleased her. And I'm sure Barbara's parents are very grateful for everyone's efforts. The people in this village really rallied round.' Doreen dabbed at her eyes.

'I'm just sorry I wasn't nicer when you first arrived. We had this idea that all you girls coming in from the towns

226

were fast and would mess about with any man you could get your hands on. But you've all knuckled down and got on with the work. And you've livened up the village.'

'I'm not sure about that. It's felt as though we have either been working or recovering from work.'

'We're all impressed and will be sorry to see you go when the time comes. Maybe you'll keep in touch and visit us.'

'I'd like that, thank you.'

Doreen joined a group of people walking over to the newly dug grave. Joe stepped forward to be beside her and then reached for her hand as the vicar started reading the burial service. As they listened to the words, the rain stopped and bright rays of sunshine pushed through the foliage of the trees.

After the family had each thrown a handful of soil onto the coffin, Doreen did the same. 'Pete says goodbye. He loved you, Barbara,' she whispered. She felt in her pocket and thought of throwing the locket and chain onto the coffin, along with Pete's letter. But it was for Barbara's parents to decide what to do with the gift he'd sent. As she broke into sobs, she felt an arm round her shoulders. Joe's tear-stained face was ashen.

★   ★   ★

It surprised Doreen when she heard laughter coming from the Drews' front room. She wanted to go in and tell everyone it wasn't right to be laughing. But wasn't that what happened at funerals? It was a chance for people to get beyond their grief and remember the person who had died by sharing stories, but get ready to carry on with their own lives. She poured tea into the cups laid out on a tray and then carried the tray, offering it first to people jammed in the hall. She returned to the kitchen to collect food to offer round. There was a good selection of sand-wiches, mainly paste and spam, but there were also some ham and some jam ones. There was a big selection of cakes. Everyone in the village had shared what rations they had, and also done without, in order to put on the best spread possible. Mr Drew had refused sugar in his tea for the past week. Doreen's eyes brimmed with tears.

'There you are. I've been looking for you.' Barbara's mother smiled at her. 'It's a good turnout. She was a popular girl. I just wish all our boys could have got back to say goodbye. And Pete. He'll be heartbroken. He was looking forward to coming home and getting married.'

'You asked me to sort out her belongings, and they're packed up ready for you to take away. Pete sent this pretty locket, which she received the day before she died.' She held it out to Mrs Booth, who touched it briefly before closing Doreen's fingers over it.

'You keep it. You were her close friend, and I know she loved you dearly from what she wrote about you in her letters.'

Doreen clutched her hand. 'We're all going to miss her, especially Joe.'

'I'm worried about him. He's taken Barbara's death badly by all accounts. We don't blame him, not one bit. We know it was an accident. We should be grateful for having had Barbara in our lives, and also remember all the good times we had with her. The life and soul of the party, was our Barbara.'

Doreen nodded in agreement.

Joe was making his way through the hall from the front room. He faltered when he saw Mrs Booth.

'Joe, come and talk to us a minute.' Mrs Booth held out a hand to him. 'I want you to understand exactly how Mr Booth and I feel. You were Barbara's friend and would never have harmed her. She wrote such nice things about you and Doreen here. She would be devastated to think you blamed yourself for what happened. Think of that, Joe Thurston. Now I want you two to look after each other. I want you to go out and enjoy yourselves. You're young, and have your lives ahead of you. Go to the pictures, go to dances. It's what Barbara would want. Do it for her.' With that, she walked away.

Joe put an arm round Doreen. He'd been tender with her before, but at that moment she felt closer to him than she'd felt to any man.

'I think you have to get over your guilt about her.' *Even if you don't get over your love for her*, she thought.

20

One evening after eating, Doreen made her excuses to Mr and Mrs Drew and went up to her room. She sat on her bed and started writing.

Dear Pete,

You asked me to tell you about Barbara's funeral. This may sound light-hearted, but she would have enjoyed it. The church was packed, the readings and hymns perfect; and when we went out to bury her, the rain stopped and the sun shone. It was as though her goodness and cheerfulness somehow filled the churchyard. The gathering was very nice, as everyone in the village produced something somehow. She was very popular. Joe blames himself for her death, which is sad.

Barbara was ever so pleased with

the locket you sent. Her mum said I was to keep it, but if you would like it back I will put it in the post. She read your letter, so knew your feelings for her, and was very happy to know you loved each other very much.

Thinking of you,
Doreen Adams

The weeks which followed were hard, but, as Mr Drew said, life had to go on. The other girls she worked with kept her going, and even Joe seemed to start recovering. Some of the girls were looking forward to going home and others wanted to stay in the country for as long as possible.

'What about you?' Joe asked one morning as they were clearing up after milking. 'Do you want to get back to London and your parents?'

'I want to stay here for as long as I can, but I'll visit them again soon. I've been thinking, Joe, about what Barbara's mum said. How we should go out and enjoy ourselves because it's what Barbara would have wanted. I thought I'd see if the others want to go to the picture house tonight. Will you come?'

'It doesn't seem right somehow.'

'We can't turn the clock back. Please, Joe, say you'll come.'

'All right. I know it's because you want a lift in the motor.' He smiled at her.

It was the first sign she'd seen of the old Joe since Barbara's death.

★ ★ ★

Arriving back at the Drews' that evening, she found a letter on the kitchen table. It was the letter she'd sent to Pete, but the address she'd written on the back had been used to return it to her. There was a scrawled note on the envelope: *Return to Sender*. She couldn't understand it, and after grabbing her purse and address book, she ran out to the phone box near the post office. Her hands were trembling as she fumbled to find the telephone number for Barbara's family.

Doreen put in her coins and pressed button A. 'Hello? Hello?'

'Hello. Who is it?' a male voice asked.

'It's Doreen, Barbara's friend from Norfolk.'

'It's Mr Booth here. Have a word with my wife.'

Doreen fed more coins into the slot as she waited. She didn't want to be cut off.

'Doreen, has something happened? Are you all right?' Mrs Booth asked.

'*I* am, but I wrote to Pete and the letter has come back unopened. I'm worried about him and thought you might know something.' The silence which followed told her what she'd already known.

'He's dead, Doreen. Shot and killed in Berlin, by one of the remaining enemy. My boys — all safe, thank God — are heartbroken. The war's over, and yet he's been killed.' With that, Mrs

Booth burst into tears.

'Hello? Mrs Booth is a bit upset. I'm sorry. Goodbye, Doreen.'

'Goodbye.' Doreen put the receiver back in its rest and leaned back against the glass panes of the kiosk.

When she walked into the Drews' kitchen, Mrs Drew took her arm and sat her down. 'I don't know what's happened, but you look as though you've had a terrible shock. I'll make some strong sweet tea and see if there's any brandy in the cupboard. We'll call it medicinal.'

Doreen felt unable to say or do anything. Barbara and Pete both dead. How would their families endure it? And all the other families who had lost someone during the war.

'There we go.' Mrs Drew put the drinks on the table in front of her then sat down. 'Do you want to tell me? You're as white as a sheet.'

'Barbara's Pete is dead. It's awful. He had to hear that she'd died, then he was killed. He must have been really

236

unhappy before he died.'

'We all find it difficult to accept our losses, but we have to keep strong. We must make the most of peace. We can't let all those lives lost fighting for peace be wasted.'

★ ★ ★

The next weeks were spent on the familiar jobs around the farm. Joe was kind to her and tried to ensure she worked with the animals. One morning, he walked into the milking parlour and leant against the wall.

'I had a dream. Barbara was in it. And you. You were messing about together like you used to, and teasing me. It gave me a good feeling. It's daft, I know, but she forgave me. Said her death was her fault as much as mine. Don't tell Dad, he'll think I'm going soft in the head. Strange though. I suddenly feel better, lighter, as though I can get on with my life.'

'I'm pleased for you, Joe.' She patted

the cow she'd been milking. 'I'll take these girls back to the field.'

'I'll walk with you.'

As they followed the cows down the lane, Doreen felt happy with Joe by her side. He was the person she considered her best friend.

'I've been wondering if you'd go out with me, Doreen. We could celebrate the end of the war. Take a picnic to the coast, walk on the beach, and forget what's been happening. What do you think?'

Doreen didn't hesitate. 'I'd love to, Joe. Do you mean just you and me? Not the other girls as well.'

'That's exactly what I mean.'

21

Doreen hadn't felt so happy in a long time. As she dressed on the morning of the seaside outing, she hummed. In the kitchen, Mrs Drew was packing a picnic for her and Joe, and had bacon and eggs ready for Doreen's breakfast.

'Tuck into that. The eggs are from Joe's farm, and the bacon . . . well, I know you don't like to know where it's come from, what with you being an animal lover.'

After finishing a mouthful of breakfast, Doreen said, 'At last everything is getting back to normal. At least for some of us.' She looked at the sun streaming in through the window and thought of Barbara and Pete.

'We must make the most of it. I have heard we may have rationing on some food for years to come. But I think we do better than they do in town.' Mrs

Drew spread jam thickly on a slice of toast. 'Mr Drew and I will miss you when you go home.'

'I feel as though this is my home now. I miss Mum and Dad and my sister and her family, but I like the people here.'

Later, as she and Joe cycled to the station, they chatted happily.

'We'll take the bikes on the train then we can go wherever we want. Let me take your bag. It's huge. Did you bring your swimming costume?'

'I did, but most of this is the picnic Mrs Drew made for us. She seems to think we're staying away for days.'

'I'd like to.' Joe looked bashful.

'What? Have a holiday?'

'Yes, but with you, Doreen. You're my best friend.'

Doreen didn't know what to say. She'd been attracted to Joe from their first meeting, but she'd had no idea he had any feelings for her. *Stop it*, she told herself. He regarded her as his friend, that was all.

They didn't talk much on the train or

the bike ride from the station. When they reached the seaside, they parked their bikes and walked down to the beach. Doreen took off her shoes and wriggled her toes into the dry sand. She loved the dunes with the tuffety clumps of grass, and she loved the sea stretching away into the distance. She stopped, breathed in deeply, and did a pirouette, stretching her arms wide. 'It's wonderful. Wonderful to be here. Wonderful to be alive. To know we're free. Come on, I'll race you to the sea.' As soon as she said it, she realised her mistake, stopped and turned.

Joe smiled at her. 'It's okay. I can still race.' With that he was off, running in a graceless sort of way.

She ran too, overtaking him, then slowing when she reached a line of crushed shells left by the tide, and then leaping through the rivulets and shallow pools, leaving indentations in the sand. She could hear Joe just behind her. When she reached the sea, she continued running, splashing through the

241

water, until it was up to her knees and her skirt hem was wet. She turned to Joe. 'Slowcoach.'

'I was simply enjoying being here. It feels good to be away from the farm after everything. I sometimes wonder if I should move somewhere else so that I can forget what happened.'

'You'd still have your memories of Barbara and that awful day. Whatever you do, wherever you go, you must remember it wasn't your fault. The only person who blames you is you.'

'I know, you're right. And I know Barbara wouldn't blame me either. But it's impossible for me to forgive myself.' They stood in silence for a while. 'How about a swim?' Joe asked. 'I can swim, but I'll have to take my leg off. Would you mind?'

'No, no I wouldn't, of course not.' But her hesitation must have worried him.

'We don't have to. It's all right.' Joe turned to make his way back up the beach.

'It wasn't your leg that made me hesitate. You'll laugh when I tell you.'

'Go on.'

'It's the thought of my swimming costume. Mum knitted me one. I've never worn it. I'm wondering how it's going to react to being in the water.'

'It might go saggy?' Joe laughed. 'We're going to look a right pair. But it doesn't matter. We can laugh at each other.'

'I wouldn't laugh at you, Joe. Not because of your leg. You know that.'

'I think I do now, but I don't want your sympathy either.' With that he was off, going as fast as he could back up to the top of the beach. Doreen stood and watched him, then followed more slowly and found a private place to change in a hollow in the dunes.

When she joined Joe on the beach, she tried not to stare at him. She was mesmerised by his body and found him very attractive. Not that she had seen many men's bodies, she reminded herself. Unable to tear her eyes from his flesh and his broad muscular frame, she felt a wave of desire pulse through her and had to divert her thoughts. 'Let's go.'

'I'll take my leg off when we're at the edge of the sea; then maybe you could give me a hand until we're in deep enough to swim.'

'Of course,' she said.

Swimming together seemed to wash all their troubles away. They didn't talk, just swam and splashed each other. When they emerged, dripping and shivering, Doreen gave a little thanks in her head for the way her costume still fitted her body and wasn't sagging down to her knees. Joe reached for her hand and held it tightly. 'Let's change and see what Mrs Drew has given us for our picnic. I'm starving.' Holding hands, they made their way back to where they had left their things.

★   ★   ★

'I want to hear all about it,' Mrs Drew said as she served up a homemade pork pie with pickled onions. 'You've a glow about you.'

'For a few hours we forgot the war, the deaths, the sadness. Joe's a good friend.'

'Still just a friend? There was no hand-holding or kissing?'

'Mrs Drew!' Doreen could feel her face flushing. 'We did hold hands, but we're just friends. He wouldn't think of me in any other way.'

'But this was a date?'

'Was it? I thought it was just two friends going on an outing.' The fact that Joe hadn't tried to kiss her had confirmed her fears.

'You want your heads knocking together. That's all I can say.'

★ ★ ★

The autumn passed with a lot of hard work and little entertainment. Occasionally, Doreen would join Joe and a few of the remaining Land Girls, along with some of the local young men who had returned from the war, on a trip to the cinema or to a local dance. They were rarely alone, and when they were, there was an awkwardness between them.

She'd received a letter from her mum asking when she'd be going home. Home? She felt at home in the country and didn't want to go back. But did she belong here? She needed to talk to someone about her future.

'Joe?' she asked as she finished mucking out the pigs. He was repairing the enclosure, as there had been a daring escape that morning by one sow and her litter.

'Mmm?' He was holding nails in his mouth. When he'd used the final one, he looked up. 'Yes, I'm all yours.'

Doreen wished that was true. 'I've been thinking about my future. My mum wants me to go home, but I like the life here. I don't know where my future is.'

'Definitely not in a pig sty!' He opened the gate, let her out and shut it securely. 'Let's sit in Mum's garden. We rarely get time to sit and talk.' He led the way into the cottage garden at the back of the farmhouse and down to the bench at the bottom. 'It's a pity Mum and Dad don't have time to enjoy it. I hope Dad retires before it's too late.'

'Will you run the farm then?'

'Yes. Whatever I said about leaving it, I don't think I could. It's been my life, always has been, always will be. I can't imagine any other work but farming. I suppose farming is in my blood.' He leant back and closed his eyes.

Doreen sat silently enjoying the colours of the late flowering shrubs. Birds darted here and there. It felt like heaven.

'What about your future, Doreen? That's what you wanted to talk about.' Joe opened his eyes and turned to her.

'I don't know. I doubt Mr and Mrs Drew want me to stay with them forever, and I don't know how much longer I'll be needed on the farms here.'

'We're short of men. I think you are

still needed on the farms. By me too. And I wondered if you'd teach me how to dance. That might take a long time.'

She laughed. 'You're a good friend, Joe.'

'And you'd never see me as anything else, would you?'

'What do you mean?'

'You wouldn't be my girlfriend?'

'Why wouldn't I?' She took his hand and stroked it gently.

'You've never shown any feelings for me like that.'

She felt her face flush. 'I did once try to kiss you. And you shouted at me.'

'I was very confused by that. At the time I thought you only kissed me because you felt sorry for me. I thought you were playing with my feelings. I felt you were making a fool of me. I liked you a lot, but feared rejection because of my disability. Later I heard about the American giving you stockings and other gifts and knew you wouldn't be interested in me. Barbara told me about him.'

'Why, Joe? Why would you think I felt sorry for you? I've liked you ever since we met. But you seemed to have fallen for Barbara. You knew she was in love with Pete, but you couldn't help yourself loving her.'

'I felt comfortable and happy with Barbara, and she made me feel worthwhile. She didn't feel sorry for me, but genuinely liked me. We laughed and had fun together. I could relax because I didn't have to create a good impression.' He took her hand. 'After our wonderful day at the seaside, my feelings for you have changed.'

Happiness spread through Doreen like the heat from a fire on a cold winter's day. Her arms wound around his neck as she pulled him towards her, enjoying the warmth of his skin. She was aware of his fingers caressing her shoulders. At last their lips met, gently at first and then with increased passion; for Doreen, it was the most wonderful sensation she had ever known.

'So are you going to tell me why you're grinning like a Cheshire cat?' Mrs Drew asked as she cut thick slices of fruitcake.

'It's Joe.'

'Hallelujah! Did you hear that, Mr Drew? Put your paper down and pay attention. Our Doreen is walking out with Joe Thurston. What did I tell you?'

'Right again,' he grunted before licking his pencil and filling in a word on the crossword.

Doreen giggled. She tried to imagine her and Joe after over forty years of marriage. Impossible. 'You were right about us needing our heads knocking together.'

'So when's the wedding to be?'

Mr Drew's head jerked up. 'Don't be ridiculous. They need time to get to know each other.'

'We do know each other, Mr Drew. I feel I know him better than anybody else in the world. Winter. We want a winter wedding. And it will be at the church here. We want to invite everyone in the village. We'll have a party in the church hall.'

'What about a dress?'

'My sister kept hers, so I'll alter it and wear something warm, a stole or something over the top.'

'You've got it all planned, then.'

Doreen giggled. 'Yes; Joe and I had a long talk about what we want after he'd asked me to marry him and I'd got over the shock. I was wondering if you'd make the cake. Like this one, which is delicious, with some pretty icing.'

Mrs Drew nodded her head then wiped away a tear with her apron. 'I can't believe it. Mr Drew, our girl is getting married.'

22

Doreen continued to work on the farms, but spent her spare time organising the wedding and cleaning up the cottage adjoining the farmhouse. It had been used by one of the farmhands who had been killed in the war, and it was tiny. Just one bedroom upstairs and one room downstairs with a kitchen at the back, but she thought it could be made nice. The toilet was outside and the bath was in the kitchen with a wooden board to put over it when not in use.

'It's a bit basic,' Joe had said when he'd first shown her round.

'Don't apologise, Joe; it's perfect. It will be special. Our first home together. I can't wait for us to move in.'

Various villagers offered bits of furniture, and Doreen and Mrs Drew sewed curtains. Not much was needed for such a tiny cottage.

Doreen became weighed down with thoughts of Barbara. On a break in the barn during a rainy morning, she opened the locket, as she often did, and stared at the images of her friend and Pete. As always, tears fell as she thought about love and how easily it could be snatched away. A shadow in the doorway made her sniff back her unhappiness, and she quickly put the locket away. When she looked again, there was nobody there.

* * *

Doreen sat at the kitchen table watching the rain lashing on the window panes. It wouldn't be long now before she was walking up the aisle with her father, the bridesmaids following, clutching their flowers. If only Barbara were here, everything would be perfect. She would have been a bridesmaid. Once again, Doreen took the locket out and opened it, sobbing as she looked at her friend's photograph. She looked so happy.

Joe's sudden appearance startled her. Doreen fumbled the locket out of sight and wiped her face with her hand.

'Hello, Joe. It's nice to see you. Come and sit next to me.'

He didn't smile and remained standing.

'What's wrong?'

'Honesty is necessary for a marriage. If you've given your heart to someone, second best isn't good enough. Our wedding is off.' Then he left, slamming the door behind him.

What had happened? That wasn't like Joe at all. Why hadn't he stayed to talk to her and to explain? What did it mean? There could only be one reason: whatever he'd said in the past, he had loved Barbara and thought Doreen was second best. Her life was shattered and she was distraught. There would be no happy ever after. She'd lost him. Too upset for tears, anguish overcame her. There would be no wedding. She'd lost the love of her life.

'We can't have this,' said Mrs Drew, bustling into Doreen's room and pulling back the curtains. 'You've been hiding yourself away for too long. I don't know what's been going on between you and Joe, but if it's as you say and the wedding's off, you need to tell people. Come downstairs and get some solid food in you first. I've cooked breakfast. I'm not taking no for an answer. Mr Drew has something to say to us both.'

Reluctantly, Doreen pulled on some clothes, did as she was told and joined Mr Drew at the kitchen table.

'If you think you're suffering, you should see Joe,' said Mr Drew.

'He called the wedding off,' snapped Doreen.

'I expect he had his reasons. Have you asked him?'

'It's obvious. From what he said, it's because he loved Barbara more than me.'

'Last night, Joe was in the pub and

had one too many. He told me he'd seen you crying over a locket, which he thinks that American chap gave you. He imagines there's a picture of Bud in it. Joe thinks your true love was Bud and you're marrying him out of pity.'

'That's ridiculous,' said Doreen, hope swelling in her heart. She *had* to find Joe.

He was sitting on a wall looking unhappy.

'Joe, it's time we talked. We seem to have been imagining all sorts of things. The locket belonged to Barbara; Pete sent it to her. Mrs Booth told me to keep it.'

Joe looked up. 'I knew Bud gave you presents and I thought that was one of them. I saw you crying over it and thought you loved him.'

'I wasn't in love with him. I felt a fraud. People were sorry for me because they thought I'd lost someone I hoped to spend the rest of my life with. I did love him, but only as a dear friend. We just wanted a good time. I'm sure it was the same for him. He never said he loved me, but we were comfortable together. And we enjoyed dancing. It made us feel free. As we danced, we forgot the war. When you saw me crying, it was about Barbara, about her and Pete. I wanted her at our wedding and it made me sad to remember they were dead. When you called the wedding off, I thought it was because you were in love with Barbara.'

'What made you think that? I only ever loved Barbara like a sister.'

'When you said about loving someone and second best wouldn't do, I thought *I* was second best.'

Joe stood and put his arms around her, pulling her close. 'You'll never be second best to me. I love you.'

'I love you, too. Will you still marry me?'

★   ★   ★

'Are your parents settled in at The White Horse all right?' Mrs Drew asked.

257

'They seem happy enough now. Mum wasn't best pleased when I first told her the wedding was going to be here. My sister and her family will be well looked after at Mrs Wright's. It was lovely of her to offer. She has a heart of gold. We didn't think that when we first met her.'

'A bit abrupt and thoughtless at times, but a good, honest woman deep down.'

Joe knocked at the door and walked in. 'Mum's sent you something, Doreen.' He handed over a blue garter. 'It's to wear at the wedding.'

'That's lovely. Please thank her.'

'Have you sorted out something old to wear tomorrow?' asked Joe.

'No.'

'I think you should wear the locket as your something old. We loved Barbara and she knew it. That's what mattered.'

'I will wear it and it will be close to my heart. Thank you, Joe. I thought I'd lost you.'

* * *

As Doreen walked up the aisle towards Joe and their future together, all she cared about was him.

The service went in a blur, but as she said the words 'I will', she touched the bodice of her dress and through the material, pressed the locket gently against her skin. Tears of happiness and hope mingled as they ran down her cheeks.

Joe took her in his arms and kissed her. Pulling away, he looked in her eyes and whispered, 'I love you, Doreen.'

Leaving the church, they were showered with confetti; and as they walked to the church hall, small children skipped and raced beside them.

'I hope you're going to dance with me, Joe.'

'I'll do my best and try not to trip up, Doreen Thurston. I expect I can manage a gentle shuffle or sway.' Joe gave her hand a squeeze. 'It's the happiest day of my life, that's for sure.'

'Mine too. And we need to put the past behind us. We have to.'

★ ★ ★

Back at their cottage that night, Doreen took Joe's hand and led him up the narrow stairs to the bedroom. She turned her back to him and he undid the fastenings and pushed the dress from her shoulders. Then he undid the clasp of the locket and laid it carefully on the dressing table. 'We need to keep that in a safe place,' he said. 'If we have a daughter, we'll give the locket to her and call her Barbara.'

23

Yvonne carried the choc ices on sticks out of the corner shop and sat on a bench next to Ivy's wheelchair. 'What a treat,' she said. 'Thank you.'

'It's me who should be thanking you,' said Ivy, licking at the ice cream. 'You are good to take me out.'

'What a beautiful afternoon. I could sit here forever,' sighed Yvonne. 'When we've finished these, I should think about collecting Susan.'

'It's best to be away before the pupils from the school over there get let out. It'll be bedlam then.'

Yvonne laughed. 'You're right. Are you ready?'

Ivy licked her lips. 'Is my mouth mucky?'

'Nothing the garden hose won't fix

when you get home,' Yvonne said with a smile.

When they arrived at Ivy's prefab, she said, 'Have you time for a cup of tea? I expect I'll make one. Oh, my goodness. John, what are you doing home?'

'Hello, Mum. Yvonne,' said John, nodding. 'I've got a few minutes between jobs and I thought I'd surprise you. Looks as if you've been gallivanting.' He winked at Yvonne.

'We had a lovely walk around the streets, looking at the pretty flowers in the gardens. Then we had an ice cream. It was a nice outing.'

'I'll say cheerio,' said Yvonne. 'I don't want to be late collecting Susan.'

Yvonne was glad to get away. She often felt awkward when John was around. She'd known him since schooldays and liked him a lot. He was a very pleasant man, but she knew he had a bit of a crush on her and didn't want to encourage him as she had no feelings for him in a romantic way. However, he was very good to Ivy, and she suspected he'd come home to check she was all right.

As she walked to the infants' school, she felt the familiar prickle of pleasure as she looked forward to seeing her daughter again. Susan had been at the school for almost a year and seemed to have settled in well. Her teacher, Miss Pringle, was a kind lady who encouraged her pupils to do the best they could.

'Mummy, here's a picture for you,' said Susan as soon as she saw Yvonne. She hurtled towards her, holding out a piece of pink paper with a crayon drawing.

Yvonne gave her daughter a hug and then inspected the picture. 'This is very good, darling. We'll hang it up on the wall in the kitchen.'

Susan pointed and said, 'That's my friend, Vivienne. Can she come to tea?'

The man with Vivienne had obviously heard what Susan said. 'Not today, I'm afraid. I'm taking her to the park.' He held out his hand to Yvonne. 'I'm Theodore Egerton and I'm Vivienne's uncle. Delighted to meet you.'

How charming he is, thought Yvonne as she told him her name. It also crossed her mind that he was very good-looking with a dazzling smile. He had neatly trimmed ebony black hair, steel-grey eyes and a full mouth. Dishy. She dismissed the thought immediately. 'Vivienne would be welcome for tea another day,' she said.

Back home, Yvonne gave Susan a glass of lemonade and a biscuit. Then they went into the garden where Yvonne half-heartedly plucked at a few weeds while Susan chatted to her.

'Vivienne wore a pretty necklace in class today. Miss said it was beautiful and it was called a liklet or something. I can't remember what she said, but it wasn't a necklace. It looked like one, though. It was gold.'

Yvonne smiled as she looked at her daughter's wide violet-coloured eyes. Her cheeks were rosy and her wavy, fair hair, a little awry after a day at school, was falling from the slide which usually anchored it off her face. Yvonne considered what Susan had said. 'Could it have been a locket?'

'Yes, I think so. What's a locket, Mummy? Why isn't it called a necklace? Does it have a lock on it?'

'Lockets are worn around your neck on a chain. They have a special opening and you can keep things inside, small things which are precious to you.' Yvonne decided not to go into the fact that a lot of lockets dated from Victorian mourning periods. 'I don't think they have a lock, but it's quite a secure place to keep things if it's working properly. Did you have a look inside?'

Susan shook her head and seemed to lose interest. 'What's for tea?'

Yvonne made ham sandwiches and opened a tin of fruit cocktail.

It was a warm evening and Susan was reluctant to go to bed. 'Please, Mummy, let me stay up a bit longer. We could play a game.'

'What about doing some of the seaside jigsaw we started yesterday? And then I'll read you two stories when you're in bed.'

'I like that jigsaw. Can we have a holiday by the sea?'

'We'll see,' said Yvonne automatically. Mentally, she worked out a few sums and decided there would be no money for holidays. Perhaps a few treats during the summer break from school, but nothing extravagant.

★   ★   ★

When Susan was in bed and Yvonne was clearing up the kitchen, she came back to the fact that she could do with an income. There was a small annuity from her late parents which they lived on, and she'd vaguely thought she might find work when Susan was at school, but she needed to be around to take her to and collect her from school, and then there were the holidays to think about. She'd put off buying a television as Susan was happy listening to *Children's Hour* on the wireless. They did have a refrigerator and a twin-tub washing machine, and they had a telephone, just in case the school needed to get in touch with her. She was very protective towards her daughter and hoped she wouldn't stifle her. The company of other people appealed to her now that Susan was away throughout the day. Idly, she wondered what work she could do, never having had a job before. She could clean, cook, wash and iron, shop. She was honest, reliable and willing, and that was about it. Where could she hope to find someone to pay her for those things? And she kept coming back to the school holidays when she had to be with Susan.

It had been a good day. Her daughter was safely in bed, hopefully dreaming pleasantly. Yvonne's thoughts drifted to Theodore Egerton. She took a deep breath and forced herself to concentrate on something else. It had been an enjoyable afternoon with Ivy and a bit of fun sitting outside the shop eating ice cream. Something Ivy had said played in her head. It had been about the school. A school! If she could get work there, she would have the holidays free to be with Susan; it was convenient to get to and . . . she'd get in touch with them the next day. With that decision made, Yvonne locked up and got ready for bed.

★   ★   ★

'You look nice, Mummy,' said Susan the following morning.

Yvonne was pleased her daughter had noticed. She'd dressed in a simple yellow and white striped sundress with a flared skirt. It complemented her mahogany eyes, and she'd brushed her brown hair until it shone. The upward flicks of hair at her jawline had gone right just for once, and she hoped it was a good omen for the morning ahead.

When they reached the school gates,

Susan ran to join a group of girls and barely gave Yvonne a wave.

'Hello, we meet again.'

Yvonne's skin prickled as she recognised the voice. 'Yes.' She turned to face Theodore. 'Did you have a nice time at the park?' She couldn't think of anything else to say and felt foolish.

'Time with Vivienne is always nice.' He sounded serious. 'My sister isn't too well at the moment, and I said I'd make sure Vivienne got to and from school without her having to worry.'

'I don't really know Vivienne or her mother, but if I can help in any way, please do ask me.'

'Can I give you a lift anywhere?' asked Theodore. 'I've got the car and I'm going into town. You might find my business interesting. We get a lot of people coming in to browse.'

'I have plans for this morning,' replied Yvonne primly.

He took her by surprise when he laughed. 'I don't close until five o'clock this afternoon. Here's my card.' With that, he jumped into his carmine-coloured sporty car. Yvonne admired its fine lines and adventurous look, but had no idea as to its make.

Not wanting to be distracted from her mission, Yvonne tucked the piece of paper Theodore had given her into her handbag and clipped it shut. She turned on her heel and started walking towards the secondary modern school. Curiosity got the better of her after a very short while and she stopped, retrieved the business card and strode purposefully into town.

She easily found the address she'd been handed. It was an old building, recently decorated in shiny black gloss paint with gold lettering depicting 'Egerton Antiques' on the outside. The windows were sparkling clean, and through them Yvonne could see Theodore. He was with a customer, and she had time to scrutinise him without him seeing her. Then, without warning, he looked up and stared at her. There was no alternative, without appearing extremely stupid, except to push open the door and walk inside.

'Good morning again,' said Theodore. 'Please have a look around. I'll attend to you when I've finished with this customer.' He turned back to the woman poring over some silver bottles. Yvonne walked to the back of the shop and pretended to be interested in some leather-bound books, running her fingers gently over the aged covers. The ambience of the shop premises was enticing, the musty aroma of things from the past, secrets buried. Yvonne's father always did say she had an imagination far too big for her. Her past life seemed to be catching up with her here in the antique shop. She felt stirrings of things which had lain hidden deeply for the past seven years.

24

'Now, I'm all yours,' murmured a voice close to her left ear. 'Did you suddenly discover you needed a book?'

Yvonne was flustered, and cross with herself for being so. She'd intended to maintain control, acting with a small degree of dignity at least. It wasn't too late to recover, she decided. 'I changed my mind, that's all. Ladies are allowed to do that, I hear.'

Theodore backed away slightly. 'Of course,' he said. 'Please continue to browse, and should you want me, please let me know.' He walked away.

Why was this man having such an effect on her? Perhaps she shouldn't have come in here. She moved around the shop slowly, looking at the various pieces on show. A tray of lockets intrigued her. Then she caught her breath and reached out to touch one; it was golden in colour, and had a floral design on the front, and when she turned it over, an engraving which resembled a church on the back. At the side was a hinge, but she felt intrusive about opening it in case there were still personal mementoes inside. Daydreaming, she wondered what they might be. What would she put inside a locket? Photographs of her parents, perhaps. Her eyes misted as she thought of them and sadness replaced her earlier joyfulness. *How transient our feelings can be,* she thought.

'Interesting, aren't they?'

Yvonne looked up, startled, having forgotten about Theodore momentarily. She gathered herself. 'Yes, very. May I ask you about a piece of jewellery Vivienne took into school? It intrigued Susan. Was it like this one?' She indicated the ornate golden locket.

Theodore shook his head. 'This is what she wore.' He held up a heart-shaped one, which even Yvonne could tell was a cheap little item. 'I've had it hanging around for a while and I let Vivienne show it off. It made her happy, although I'm not sure her teacher approved of her wearing jewellery to school.' He frowned, but his displeasure was short-lived and soon a smile appeared. 'Tell me what brings you to see me.'

'You invited me, remember?' Yvonne was indignant and wasn't happy with the idea that Theodore thought she was chasing him.

He laughed at her. 'I'm only teasing you.' His eyes danced.

'I think you've a fascinating shop,' deflected Yvonne, 'but I won't be buying anything.'

Theodore raised his eyebrows. 'Don't you like the look of my stock? Of course, old things aren't to everyone's taste.'

'It's not that,' said Yvonne, feeling uncomfortable. 'I don't have any money to buy anything other than necessities.' She wouldn't dream of wasting her savings on items from this shop even if they were exquisite.

Theodore remained silent and Yvonne wondered what he was thinking. She was also wondering why she'd mentioned money. Then he said, 'I could offer you a job here if you like, if your husband won't mind.'

'What sort of job?' She ignored the part about a husband. 'I know nothing about antiques, and my book-keeping skills aren't up to much. What could I do?'

'I don't know. Perhaps display the stock to full advantage; group things together which might interest a buyer into looking at something they wouldn't have considered otherwise. For example, a book about the seventeenth century with some curios from that era.'

'But I know nothing about things like that,' protested Yvonne, although she was already feeling persuaded.

Theodore gazed deeply into her eyes and said, 'But you could learn.'

'I'll think about it,' she breathed.

Theodore looked at his watch. 'Will

you join me for coffee? I hate going to cafés on my own.'

'A drink would be nice. Thank you.'

Yvonne thought they would go across the road to the Kardomah café, so was surprised when Theodore opened the passenger door of his car which was parked outside the shop and put out a hand to help her in. 'Where are we going?' she asked.

'Wait and see.' He grinned, noisily revving the engine, and pulling away from the kerb.

It was exhilarating to feel the breeze through her hair, but she would look a wreck when they got to wherever it was they were going. She registered they were heading towards the countryside. The trees were a blur and the sky flashed by as she looked up. Where were they? She tried to ask Theodore, but he didn't respond except to cover her hand with his own, and she briefly enjoyed its warmth before tugging it away. Then abruptly, the car swung to the left and slowed down.

'I thought we could have something to eat. I'm well-known here, and thought you'd like to see the place.' Theodore indicated a large hotel in front of them.

Yvonne was furious. 'How dare you bring me here without asking if it was all right! I thought we were going for a coffee somewhere in town.'

Yvonne grabbed the handle and wrested open the door. Theodore said, 'It crossed my mind we might enjoy a steak meal. We could eat on the terrace and admire the garden.'

'I don't want to eat with you. I don't even want to have coffee with you now. In fact I want nothing to do with you. Now take me home, or I'll — '

Theodore looked at her with a shocked expression on his face, and Yvonne sagged against the car. Did he really pose a threat? She supposed not, but he had frightened her, and she had lost control of the situation once again, which made her annoyed. 'You took me by surprise, that's all.' Then, calming down, she said, 'Anyway, isn't it a little early for steak?'

'I'm sorry, I shouldn't have whisked you out of town without warning. I should have asked you. As we're here, I can give you a tour of the grounds if you like. They're quite extensive and beautiful. At least, I think so. And then you can decide if we stay for lunch.'

The rest of the morning passed very pleasantly for Yvonne. It was a change from household jobs, and adult company was very welcome. Not that she didn't enjoy being with Ivy, but her conversation was somewhat limited. Also, Yvonne conceded, she enjoyed being in male company. And Theodore Egerton was definitely all male.

Later, sitting on the terrace of The Lawns Hotel, Yvonne said, 'What a delicious meal. How do you know this place? Are you a regular customer?'

'I own a share in it,' replied Theodore. 'And, yes, I *am* a regular customer. I've a flat here. I live alone, can't cook and refuse to learn.'

'I suppose there's no need to learn when you can order what you fancy from this restaurant,' said Yvonne, thinking of the baked beans on toast and boiled ham dinners she regularly dished up.

'My sentiments exactly. Now, I think I'd better get back to work or my assistant will feel put upon. He's only part-time and is due to leave soon. Are you ready? I'll take you home.'

'Please drop me at your shop,' said Yvonne. 'I need to walk off the food.' She stood up before asking, 'Were you serious about the job offer?'

'Very serious. But I don't want to make life complicated for you at home. Have a chat with your husband and let me know.'

⋆　⋆　⋆

Yvonne was exhausted when she got home. Her mind was reeling with the events of the day so far. Theodore Egerton was a very attractive man. She thought he was attracted to her, but couldn't be sure. Perhaps he was buttering her up because he needed a display assistant or whatever the position was called. She had been rather amused at his references to her husband, but she wouldn't bring up the subject unless she needed to. It dawned on her that the school holidays hadn't been mentioned, nor had the hours of work. It would mean another trip to his antique shop during the week, unless she saw him at the school gates.

After a cursory tidy of the house, Yvonne decided to call on Ivy.

'Ivy, I've brought the material for the pinafore dress I'm making for you. It's a bit warm for a fitting, but it's tacked together.'

'And what else was it you wanted, Yvonne?' asked Ivy, filling the kettle and opening the biscuit tin. 'I've known you a long time, and I can tell there's something on your mind.'

Yvonne sighed. 'You're right, of course. Well, I was going to go to the school over the road from the shop and ask if they had any suitable vacancies. Anyway, the short of it is that I didn't get that far. I went into town and . . . ' Here she diverted the story a little. ' . . . called in to have a look around the antique shop in Parade Terrace. I spoke to the owner and he offered me a job there. It was quite unexpected.'

'So what's the catch? You don't seem very satisfied with the outcome.'

Yvonne carried the tea tray through to the sitting room and they sat down. 'It's just that I need something which will fit around Susan. I can't work in the holidays and I was so surprised at the offer of a job, I didn't think to mention it. Anyway, it can be easily fixed. I'll go back tomorrow and see what he says.'

'Do you want the job?' asked Ivy.

'I think so. I want a job, anyway. I need extra money and grown-up company. I think I'm rather naïve in a lot of ways. I want to broaden my experience of life outside the home. I'm beginning to feel stifled.' Yvonne breathed in sharply. What had she said? 'Not that — '

'It's all right, dear, I do understand that you don't see many people other than me and sometimes John. I think a job would be good for you. You should be with people your own age. Unless this man is as old and decrepit as me.'

'Oh, Ivy, I shouldn't have come here this afternoon. I'm being extremely insensitive without even trying.'

'I could have Susan, you know. In the holidays. If you decide to take the job. She's a dear little girl and I think we get on well.'

'I couldn't let you do that,' said Yvonne, at the same time thinking what a suitable solution that would be. 'It would be far too much of an undertaking for you.'

'The offer's there, just remember that.' Ivy dunked a digestive biscuit into her tea and sucked on it. 'Drink up, and then shall we see if this dress is going to fit me or if I'll have to give up biscuits?'

When it was time for Yvonne to leave Ivy and collect Susan from school, she felt much more settled and calm about her future. Even if she decided against the job with Theodore, there was still the safety net of Ivy looking after Susan if she were to look for a different job.

Theodore was nowhere to be seen when Yvonne arrived at the school. Susan waved to her and they started the walk home.

'Vivienne was sent home from school today,' said Susan. 'She fainted. Fell straight to the floor and didn't get up. We thought she was dead. But she wasn't.'

'Poor Vivienne,' replied Yvonne. 'I hope she feels better soon.' Then she found herself asking, 'Did her uncle come and collect her?'

'I don't know. Someone took her out of the classroom, and Miss Pringle told us to be quiet and sit down and carry on with our reading.'

Susan chattered as they walked home, but Yvonne wasn't giving her as much attention as usual. Her thoughts were on Theodore. She formed a plan in her mind, and when they arrived at their house, she said, 'It will soon be the school holidays. You won't have to go to school for six weeks.'

'What will I do, then? Stay at home with you? Will we go to the park and have a swing?'

'That's a good idea. And we can visit Ivy. You like being with her, don't you?' Yvonne felt a bit mean, but she wanted to know that if the occasion did arise, Susan would be happy with Ivy looking after her.

'Yes, I like her. I like John as well.'

'They're good people. Now, let's have some orange squash and then you can play in the garden if you like.'

While Susan was playing a game of make-believe, Yvonne was thinking hard about what working alongside Theodore Egerton would be like. He was definitely handsome and appeared to have a lifestyle similar to a film star what with owning an antique business, a share in a large prestigious hotel and actually living there. There was a niggle at the back of her mind that perhaps it might be better to see if she could get a job at the school and use the offer from Theodore as a standby plan. She thought about it for a while — a very short while — and then decided she didn't want to. Theo's offer of a job was something exciting to look forward to. Now she was going to make sure she came first for once.

25

Without giving herself time to think, Yvonne pushed open the door and heard the tinkling of the bell as she stepped into Egerton Antiques. Her heart pattered more quickly than usual, which she put down to nerves, but she knew it was happiness and anticipation at seeing Theodore again.

'May I be of assistance?'

Yvonne found herself face to face with a middle-aged man with greying hair. 'I was hoping to speak to Theodore Egerton,' she said.

'I'm sorry, madam, but he's out on business.'

'I don't suppose you could tell me what time he's expected back.'

'He didn't say, madam, but he'll definitely be here by three o'clock this afternoon. That's when I finish for the day. Will you come back, or can I give him a message?'

'I'll come back. Please tell him Yvonne Mitchell called to see him. Thank you.' And she swept out of the shop.

It was a perfect summer day and the park beckoned. Yvonne treated herself to a brick ice cream and licked it while she walked around the bandstand.

'Hello,' said a voice which immediately had her in a nervous state. A big blob of ice cream landed on the bodice of her dress and she felt her face flare. 'Ideal day for ice cream.' Theodore was making fun of her again.

'Yes,' she agreed. 'I seem to be dripping mine rather than eating it though.' She licked the vanilla rectangle slowly. Then she said, 'I called in to see you, but you weren't there. I was concerned when Susan said Vivienne was unwell at school yesterday. How is she feeling?'

'She's a lot better, thank you. I think she was rather anxious about her mother.' He hesitated before going on,

287

'I can give you my sister's address if you like. She would enjoy a visit from you, I'm sure.'

'Yes, please,' said Yvonne. 'I would like to meet her.' She finished the ice cream and wiped her mouth with a handkerchief. 'I also wanted to ask you about the job you said I might be able to do. I have to consider Susan, and I didn't clarify that it would have to be a bit flexible as there will be school holidays to consider.'

'That wouldn't be a problem. I'm sure we could work something out. Have lunch with me next week and we'll talk more, what do you say?'

'Yes, all right. Thank you.' Her insides danced around with the ice cream, making her feel slightly sick.

On her way home, Yvonne decided she would make the detour and see if Vivienne's mother was at home. King's Avenue was delightful. Suddenly, the small house in the dreary terrace where they lived now seemed unappealing. If the job at the antique shop turned out as she hoped it would, that could be her stepping stone into a larger, more affluent and interesting world. Surprised by her thoughts, as she had never been a materialistic sort of person, she wondered what lay ahead.

The door of the large detached house was opened by an attractive woman with a blonde bubble-cut hairstyle. She looked remarkable in a geometric shift dress of varying shades of ochre and sienna. 'Are you Vivienne's mother? My daughter is in her class at school. I'm Yvonne Mitchell.'

'Oh, please come in. I've heard so much about Susan, and my brother has mentioned you. I'm Cordelia Warren, but please call me Delia.'

Yvonne followed her through a cool hallway to a pleasant sunny room overlooking a beautifully maintained garden. 'What a lovely house you have,' she said. 'I just called to ask how you are feeling and if there is anything I can do to help. Theodore mentioned you'd been unwell. Also, I understand Vivienne was poorly yesterday.'

'Vivienne's fine today, thank you. I'm sure it was the heat.' Delia frowned. 'Theo fusses. Let's have some iced tea and a gossip, and then we can go to the school together to collect the children. Please say you will. I like Fridays, don't you?' said Delia. 'A nice weekend ahead with nothing special to get up for. Perhaps we could meet, have a picnic. What do you say?'

Delia's company was vibrant, and she was sure Susan would enjoy playing with Vivienne instead of the rather dreary weekend she'd vaguely planned for the two of them. 'It sounds marvellous. Are you sure you're up to it? I don't want your husband or brother to tell me off for causing you to overdo things.'

'I'm fine. I just get a bit unhappy at times. Theo thinks I'm depressed.' She pulled a face. 'Truly, I'm fine, especially now I've got a new friend.'

★   ★   ★

Yvonne knew she couldn't compete with Delia's fashionable clothes, so she didn't even try. Together she and Susan prepared cheese and pickle sandwiches, sardine paste rolls and cut chunks of fruitcake, packing everything into a basket ready to go to the park for their picnic.

'This will be the best Saturday I've ever had, Mummy,' sighed Susan. 'I love Vivienne, and her mum is very pretty, isn't she?'

'She is. And so are you,' laughed Yvonne, bending down to pop a kiss on Susan's nose. 'Come on, let's go.'

The four of them had a wonderful time, chatting and playing catch, and hitting a ball to one another; then the children went round and round on the roundabout and back and forth on the swings. The sun followed them, and soon they were pink with exertion and sunrays. Yvonne sank to the grass, complaining, 'I shall have to stop. I need a rest.'

'Poor old thing,' sympathised Delia,

flopping down beside her, calling the children. She crawled towards the picnic baskets and pulled out a square of greaseproof paper. 'Food — that's what we need, Yvonne. Can't remember what's in this package, but help yourself.'

The salmon and cucumber bridge rolls made Yvonne's picnic look meagre. She bit into one. It was delicious. They were all quietly eating until Vivienne announced she was thirsty. Yvonne hauled herself up and said, 'I'll get us some cartons of orange squash from the kiosk, shall I? Or shall we go to the cafeteria and get some cups of tea?'

Delia rolled onto her back and stretched out her arms behind her. 'I can't move,' she declared, 'unless someone wants to carry me.' She closed her eyes and the girls giggled at her.

'This is the best day I've ever had,' said Susan.

'Me, too,' agreed Vivienne. 'Oh, look, I can see Uncle Theo!' Mummy, it's Uncle Theo!' She stood up and waved. 'Here we are.'

'I'm getting us all a drink,' said Yvonne.

'I'll come with you,' said Theo, standing so close to her she could feel the heat of his body through the fibre of his cotton shirt on her bare arm, and smell his light citrus cologne.

Together they strolled to the refreshment pavilion.

'I can't stay long,' said Theo. 'I thought I'd pop along and see if you girls were having a good time. It looks like it, I must say. Delia looks happier than I've seen her in a long while.'

She looked up into his eyes and caught her breath. He was striking. A thought came to her: he said he lived alone, but he must have a girlfriend. She'd find out from Delia.

Theo walked back to the playground with Yvonne and said his farewells.

'He's nice, isn't he?' said Susan, sucking at her squash from the frozen triangular cardboard container. 'Can we have a boat ride, please?'

'We'll see,' said Yvonne automatically.

'That means no,' whispered Susan to Vivienne. The children shrugged and helped themselves to butterfly cakes which Delia had packed, then they started chatting happily together.

'They get on well,' remarked Delia, lighting a cigarette. She reached for her bag. 'Here, I've a present for you.'

Yvonne gasped when she saw what it was. 'I couldn't possibly accept that.' She stared at the gold locket she'd seen in the antique shop.

'Why ever not? Oh, will your husband object? Think you've a bit on the side?' She winked at Yvonne and smiled. 'Theo brought it over for me when he visited last night. Thought it would cheer me up. To tell the truth, I don't much like it, but he mentioned you were fascinated by it, so I thought I'd give it to you. Do you really like it?'

'I do like it. And I was taken with it in your brother's shop, but it's far too expensive an item for me to accept as a gift.' Then she laughed. 'That's a silly thing to say, as I've no idea how much it's worth. It just seems a very special, and therefore expensive, item.' She couldn't keep her eyes off the tantalising design on the front and turned it over to gaze upon the image of the church again. It was like a magnet, drawing her to it.

'And your husband won't mind?' persisted Delia.

Yvonne lay alongside her new friend and whispered, 'I haven't got one. Please don't let's talk about it in front of the children.'

Delia became very serious. 'Oh my goodness, I'm sorry. I had no idea.' Then a little smile pulled at the corners of her mouth. 'What an intrigue. You arc full of surprises, Yvonne Mitchell. Put the locket in your bag and we'll say nothing more until we are alone.'

26

Yvonne found she was almost as pleased to see Delia at the school gates on Monday morning, dropping off Vivienne, as she would have been if Theo had been there. She was thrilled to have made a friend, and although she didn't know much about her, Yvonne felt at ease with her.

'Now, let's go somewhere for coffee and you can tell me all about your non-husband,' said Delia, linking arms with Yvonne.

Yvonne was about to suggest they go back to her house, but it seemed so shabby after Delia's posh home. 'We could go out to The Lawns Hotel. Do you know it?'

'As a matter of fact, I do. That's where Theo lives.' Delia laughed. 'I know you're teasing me. Theo told me you had a rendezvous there.'

'It will have to be the little café at the back of the cake shop in Station Road, then. Will that be all right?'

'Perfect.'

Sipping frothy coffee and nibbling on shortbread fingers, Yvonne and Delia chatted about their daughters, the school, the latest fashions, and their hobbies. Then Delia drained her cup, wiped the foam from her mouth with a serviette, and said, 'I'll order another coffee and then you can tell me all about your non-husband.' She put her hand on Yvonne's. 'If you'd rather not, I will understand. But I am intrigued and nosy.'

'His name is Ted,' began Yvonne. It had been a while since she'd thought of him. She wanted to tell her new friend about him; it would be a release.

'I was at school when I met him. To me he was the most handsome man in the world. He asked me to marry him. Mum and Dad said I had to take my exams first, but they could tell I wouldn't be put off. We spent as much time as we could together, and of course the inevitable happened. I thought it was wonderful — well, to tell you the truth, I thought it was *awful*.' Delia giggled. 'Anyway, awful or not, I was pregnant. I thought *that* part was wonderful, and was overjoyed. Mum and Dad weren't too happy and neither was Ted. Said he hadn't expected to be a father and didn't want to be one either. Was blowed if he'd be lumbered with a baby. He just walked away. Didn't even say goodbye. I never saw him again.' Yvonne glanced at Delia and saw her eyes glittering. 'Mum and Dad were marvellous. They saw me through the pregnancy and birth and let me and Susan live with them. They insisted I didn't hide away or feel ashamed. They didn't even make a fuss when I said I didn't want to take my exams. All they asked was that I called myself Mrs Mitchell, that's the family name. But do you know what the saddest thing was? My parents died soon after Susan was born. They didn't get to know her.' Tears dribbled down Yvonne's cheeks and she had to sip some coffee to unblock her constricted throat. 'That's it. That's the story of the non-husband.' She gave a wobbly smile.

'Oh, Yvonne. How very wretched. I shouldn't have asked. I've wrenched every last emotion out of you. Poor you.'

But Yvonne was pleased to have put the story into words. Ivy and John knew, of course, having been friends of the Mitchell family for all of Yvonne and John's lives. But no one else knew; she hadn't told a soul. She grinned at Delia, then slid her fingers to her neck and held out the gold locket. 'I love it, thank you.'

With the atmosphere lightened, Delia paid the bill and the two of them decided to go shopping. Yvonne explained she hadn't any money and, contrary to expectations, Delia said, 'Well you can watch me spend mine!' Yvonne was very pleased she hadn't offered to buy her something or give or lend her some money. She would much rather watch Delia shopping. Besides, she had something much more precious. It seemed that every time she touched the locket, there was a link with something, but she had no idea what it was.

To Yvonne, Delia was a whirlwind, darting into this shop and then that shop, picking up clothes, handbags and shoes; the list seemed endless. In one shop she selected a midnight-blue beaded mini-dress which she tried on and paraded in front of Yvonne. 'What do you think?'

'It's beautiful,' replied Yvonne. 'And you look super in it.'

'We'll go out for a meal. You, me, Theo and my husband, Harry. No arguments, I'll fix it up.'

Yvonne kept quiet. She wouldn't go, of course. For one thing, she had nothing to wear which would match the occasion, and for another, she had Susan to look after.

★   ★   ★

'Hello.'

The voice sent a shockwave through Yvonne as she heard Theo behind her. She turned and said, 'Oh, I hope Delia is all right.'

'She's fine. I just wanted to see you. I haven't the foggiest idea where you live and I don't have your telephone number. How can I get in touch with you without them, except by trailing over here to the local infants' school?'

'Is it about the job?'

'Oh, you can have the job if you like. What I want is to take you out for a meal. I said so. didn't I? And Delia has kept on about the four of us meeting up at The Lawns. She's also told me there's no Mr Mitchell around to sock me on the jaw for wanting to take you out. So, there's no escape for you, I'm afraid. Shall we say this coming Friday? Here, write down your contact details and Delia and Harry will pick you up at seven o'clock. I hope that's all right with you. I must hurry or I'll be late for work, and that would never do!'

In a haze, Yvonne did as she was told, handed the piece of paper and pen back to Theo, and watched as he strode off back to his car. Then she wondered what Delia had said about Ted. Not too much, she hoped. But what was said couldn't be unsaid, she thought.

It seemed to Yvonne that if she was to work for Theo in the antique shop, she would have to get used to a more erratic lifestyle. She *would* go out with them on Friday and she wouldn't feel ashamed of her house. It wasn't long since Ivy had offered to look after Susan, and her daughter had indicated she'd be happy in Ivy and John's company. All she had to do now was visit Ivy and make the arrangements.

As she'd hoped, Ivy was delighted with the fact that Susan would be sleeping at her home on Friday night. Yvonne had couched the arrangements as part social and part job-related.

When Yvonne arrived home, the telephone was ringing, a rare occurrence. It was Delia. 'Theo gave me your number. We've a babysitter coming along to look after Vivienne on Friday evening. Why don't you bring Susan over? They'd love a night together, wouldn't they?'

'I've already got a babysitter,' said Yvonne, not willing to be swayed from her own planning.

'Cancel her, then,' said Delia.

'No, I think it's better if I leave things as they are, but thank you all the same. I'll see you at seven on Friday. I'm looking forward to it.' She replaced the handset and let out a breath.

Now she must sort out something to wear. All she had in the way of summer outfits were a few tired and worn sundresses and a couple of skirts, pairs of trousers and blouses. None of those would be suitable. Then she remembered she'd kept a few of her mother's clothes, things she couldn't bear to part with. Among them she found a boat-necked emerald-green cocktail dress with a black flocked lace overlay. Her mother had worn it several times to Yvonne's father's office parties. It brought a good memory, one which gave her confidence. She held the dress to her face and inhaled. A faint smell of lily of the valley came to her, which was strange, as her mother never used that as a perfume because it gave her a headache, but she loved the flowers growing outside the back door. As quickly as the scent materialised, it vanished. Yvonne hung the dress on the outside of her wardrobe, where she hoped the few creases would ease out, ready for Friday.

She'd made a start at directing her life along the path she wanted it to go.

27

Delia was a bit frosty towards Yvonne on Friday evening. She knew it was because she hadn't given in to the babysitting plans, and as the evening progressed, Delia mellowed. Yvonne had a small glass of sweet sherry before the meal, but stuck to orange juice while she was eating. She noticed the men had a glass of wine each, but Delia had a few glasses of wine throughout the evening after having a cocktail at the bar on their arrival. Harry was great fun, teasing Delia, complimenting Yvonne and giving Theo advice he asked for. The meal of prawn cocktail, roast lamb and black forest gateau was delicious. 'You are very lucky to live here, Theo,' Yvonne said.

'I'm glad you like the place. We could have a look around if you want to.'

'Yes, Theo, show Yvonne your home,' Delia said with a smile. 'I'm sure she'd like to see it. Harry and I can go to the lounge bar and have a nightcap, can't we, darling?' She leant over and kissed her husband's cheek.

'I don't think you need a nightcap, do you? Perhaps a coffee.'

As Theo walked beside Yvonne along the corridor to his flat, he said, 'You look especially pretty tonight. What a beautiful dress. It suits you very well. And I've noticed you're wearing the necklace. Do you like it?'

Yvonne's fingers flew to her throat and grasped the locket. 'Yes. Do you mind that I'm wearing it?' She felt very uncomfortable.

'Why should I mind? Although I gave it to Delia, I didn't really think it was her sort of thing. When she told me she'd passed it to you, I was pleased. You and it go together somehow. Call it antique dealer's intuition. Now, this is the entrance to my humble abode.'

'It's very grand,' said Yvonne, after being given a tour of the three-bedroom flat. 'Am I right in thinking there's no wife or girlfriend around?'

Theo shook his head. 'None. Is that what you wanted to hear?'

Yvonne wouldn't be drawn. She kept quiet, pleased with the answer he'd given her, and considered his home. The décor was a bit too ornate for her taste, but it wasn't her place, it was Theo's. There were two large settees in the sitting room facing each other, with a coffee table between them. 'It looks like something out of a magazine.'

'Is that good or bad?' asked Theo, a smile playing on his lips.

'It's different from what I'm used to,' admitted Yvonne.

'Very diplomatic.' Then he put an arm around her shoulder, gazed deeply into her eyes and brought his lips to hers in a surprising kiss. Yvonne was shocked by the extent of her feelings. She reached her arms around his neck and kissed him back, wanting to stay with him in this embrace forever. He pulled away. 'That was nice,' he said.

Nice? She had never been so

insulted, but wouldn't own up to her feelings. 'Yes. Should we be getting back to Delia and Harry? I've had a *nice* evening, but I'd like to go home now.' Her face felt hot and her voice was not quite steady.

'I've offended you,' said Theo. He seemed on the verge of saying more, but hesitated before adding, 'Yes, you're right, it's time to go.'

★   ★   ★

Delia was leaning back on a plush velvet chair, sipping at a drink. On the table beside her, a bottle of champagne sat, half empty. Her speech was a little slurred, and when she saw Yvonne and Theo, she beckoned them over. 'One for the road,' she called. 'Come on, hurry up or there won't be any left. Harry, order another bottle.'

Theo's face was set very seriously as he took in the scene. 'Harry, you take Delia home, I'll make sure Yvonne gets back all right. I've only had one glass of wine this evening, so I can drive her.'

Harry nodded. 'Sorry,' he said. 'I thought it was all going well.'

Yvonne wasn't sure what was happening, but she knew now was not the time to ask or to argue. She collected her coat, said goodbye to Delia and Harry, and followed Theo out to his car.

'So you can see what her problem is now.' Theo ran his fingers through his hair. 'What a mess.'

'Does Delia like a drink or two?' asked Yvonne.

'Or two would be fine.' Theo let out a breath. 'You don't want to be involved in our family problems. In you get; I'll have you home in no time.'

So that was it. Delia's illness. Yvonne could only feel sympathy for all of the people involved, especially Vivienne. Every family had skeletons jangling around in cupboards.

'Would you like to come in?' she asked Theo when he pulled up outside her front gate.

'What? Oh, sorry, miles away.' Then a grin softened his features. 'I've shown you mine, now I get to see yours, is that it?'

About to make an indignant reply, Yvonne saw the funny side and laughed. 'Something like that. I'll make coffee. I think we could both do with some, don't you?'

By the time they'd nearly finished their second cups, they were chatting easily. 'I think you've a lovely cosy nest here, Yvonne. I'm sure you and Susan are happy in this house.' He put his cup down and moved towards her. 'I think we've a bit of unfinished business, if you've forgiven me for being insensitive.' Again his lips brushed hers, his hands caressed her cheeks and moved down towards her naked shoulders. She leaned into him and held him tightly.

★   ★   ★

When Theo had gone, Yvonne changed into her nightdress and put away her finery. She mulled over everything that had gone on that evening. There was so much to think about, some good, some not so good. As she washed the coffee cups, she realised she hadn't been alone in the house at night since Susan had been born. It felt quite liberating, she admitted to herself reluctantly. It was probably time she was in bed, but she didn't feel tired and knew she wouldn't sleep. She sat in the sitting room with her feet up on a pouffe and fingered her necklace, which she still wore.

If she were going to look at the inside of the locket, now was the time to do it, she decided. She was able to prise it open quite easily and held her breath as she took out the contents.

The lock of hair didn't surprise her, nor the smiling faces of lovers gazing at each other, and she was enchanted with the drawings. Yvonne darted up to her bedroom and took out a box from the bottom of her chest of drawers. In it, she kept important papers and some photographs of her parents. She found the one she was looking for and held it up in front of her. It was of a newborn Susan being cuddled by her grandmother with a proud-looking grandfather looking on. It would be perfect for the locket. She trimmed it to size with needlework scissors and tried to fit it in, but it proved difficult. Hoping she hadn't ruined the photograph, she tried again. This time, with a little more trimming, it fitted the space perfectly. She was pleased with the result and closed the locket, clipping it around her neck again. Perhaps she would always wear it, never take it off. The idea pleased her and she thought there was a faint smell of lily of the valley. She laughed as she remembered again her father's words about her power of invention.

★ ★ ★

After a pleasant and dreamless sleep, Yvonne woke at nine o'clock the next morning and got ready to pick up Susan.

When she arrived, her daughter was hiding under some sort of contraption draped with blankets.

John was laughing at her and waved to Yvonne. 'Mum's in the kitchen, go straight in. She'll be pleased to see you.'

'Tea's ready,' said Ivy, handing a cup to Yvonne. 'Let's go into the sitting room and you can tell me all about last night.'

Yvonne had no intention of doing quite that, but she entertained Ivy with details of the meal and the surroundings. 'It's a beautiful place, Ivy. You should get John to take you there one day.'

'Not quite his style. He prefers a café with big mugs of strong tea and a good fry-up. He won't change, even for the Queen of England.'

'Ivy, you know a bit about flowers, don't you? You're always naming the ones we see in the gardens when we go for our walks. Do you know anything about lily of the valley?'

'It's a pretty flower. I remember your

mother liking it, but it gave her terrible headaches if she had the perfume near her. Why do you ask?'

Yvonne showed Ivy the locket. 'I can smell lily of the valley sometimes. It's very strange. It's not just with the locket and its association with the flower. The dress I wore last night was one which had belonged to Mum. I got the same fleeting aroma from that, and as you say, she wouldn't have had the perfume around her. I can't explain it at all.'

Ivy was quiet for a minute. Then she said, 'There's a language of flowers, Yvonne. I don't know if you've heard of it.' Yvonne shook her head. 'It's what each flower means. I'm sure I'm right in saying that lily of the valley symbolises the return of happiness.' Yvonne sat rigid before a tremor ran through her body. Could it be possible? It wasn't likely that she should experience something as ghostly as that. No locket could possess those powers. Ivy laid a hand on hers and said, 'Let's hope it's true. You deserve happiness if anyone does.'

Yvonne felt ridiculous being so affected by something as ethereal as a scent. 'You're very kind, Ivy. Thank you.'

'Anyway, little Susan was no trouble at all. I think she liked staying with us, and as you can see, John's very taken with her. They've got a secret hideaway made out of the clothes horse and some old blankets. I often wondered if you and John would hit things off together. I think he'd like it if the three of you could make a little family.'

'He's a good man, and I've known him all my life, but I've never felt like that towards him. Oh dear, Ivy, I didn't want to cause any awkwardness. Perhaps I shouldn't have asked you to have Susan.' Yvonne was flustered, not wanting to offend Ivy.

'Nonsense! It was one of the best evenings we've had. Please say she can stay again.' Ivy looked near tears.

Yvonne thought rapidly. 'Yes, of

course.' It fitted in with her sudden half-formed plans. 'How about next weekend? Would Saturday be all right?'

'I'll check with John, but that sounds fine. Susan could come here mid-morning and we could have a lovely day and night with her. John will be pleased.'

'I'm sure Susan will be, too.' *And so shall I,* thought Yvonne.

With the tea finished, and the game in the garden ended, Yvonne and Susan sauntered home in the sunshine. 'I'm pleased you had a good time, Susan. Would you like to visit Ivy and John next weekend?'

'And stay for the night?' asked Susan, her shining face turned towards Yvonne, who nodded. 'Yes please.'

At home, Susan ran into the garden with some toys. Yvonne picked up the phone and dialled a number. 'Hello, it's Yvonne,' she said. 'Theo, I wondered if you would like to come over for a meal on Saturday evening.'

'I'd like that very much.'

'Shall we say seven o'clock? It will be

a very informal evening.'

'I'm looking forward to seeing Susan again,' said Theo.

'She won't be here. She's spending the day and night with friends.'

The telephone conversation ended, and Yvonne hoped she could follow through her intentions of having an intimate evening with Theodore Egerton.

28

So far, Yvonne had evaded telling Ivy what she was up to over the weekend, but she knew she'd have to let on at some time. Susan hadn't asked why she was spending the night with Ivy and John, all she did was say how much she was looking forward to it.

What would cook easily so she could spend time with Theo? She wished she was daring enough to make a curry meal, which she'd heard was the fashionable thing to do. A bottle of Blue Nun and one of Mateus Rosé were sitting in the refrigerator, but that was as far as her preparations had progressed. Concentrating hard, she came up with a menu of melon balls with glacé cherries and a pinch of ginger, beef goulash, followed by banana splits which could be made quickly after the main course had been eaten.

The week flew by and at last it was Saturday. Yvonne walked an excited Susan to Ivy's. 'Will you be all right on your own, Mummy?'

'I won't be on my own the whole time. I've got someone coming to dinner.' Yvonne knew she had to tell Susan who it was, and there was no reason to keep it a secret. 'It's Theo. He's coming over to keep me company.'

'I haven't seen Vivienne in school for a few days. Do you think she's not well?'

'I can ask Theo and let you know. Now let's go and say hello to Ivy and John.'

They were welcomed like long-lost family. John had bought some comics and a book for Susan and he was trying hard to hide a bar of Five Boys, a tube of spangles and something wrapped in a white paper cone.

'Are we allowed to know what you're doing this evening?'

'Mum, we mustn't pry,' protested John, but his face was pink and he didn't look at her.

'Theo's coming for dinner,' said Susan. 'Shall we play hide and seek in the garden?'

It seemed as if John couldn't wait to get outside. Yvonne had a knack of upsetting him, but there was nothing she could do about it.

'Am I allowed to know who Theo is?' asked Ivy, her eyes bright.

'He's the uncle of a friend of Susan's. The one I had a meal with last weekend, when Susan stayed here.'

'And he's taking you out again this weekend? He sounds keen.' Ivy's head cocked to one side like a little robin.

'It's not quite like that,' replied Yvonne. 'I'm cooking him a meal.'

Ivy put her hand on Yvonne's arm and said, 'Make sure you enjoy yourself. It's about time you had a life of your own.'

★ ★ ★

The table in the dining room was laid by early afternoon. Yvonne had chosen an embroidered cloth her mother had made and she'd added white linen napkins. Then she prepared the melon and put it in the refrigerator, before putting together the goulash. A short while later delicious aromas were coming from the saucepan, but it was getting really hot in the kitchen. All she had to do now was to leave it to cook on a low heat — and not forget it.

Yvonne changed into a simple honey-coloured shift dress which she'd made, and everything else was as ready as it could be.

Bang on seven o'clock the doorbell rang, and there was Theo. Yvonne noticed again how gorgeous he was.

'I've brought you some chocolates.' He handed over a box of Terry's of York chocolate assortment.

'Thank you.'

'I must tell you what's been happening. Harry has decided to change his job after being offered a different post a little while ago. He's moved the family to the coast, near Cromer. Delia will be going into a residential centre where they will try to stop her drinking, and Vivienne will either go to boarding school or have a live-in housekeeper to take care of her when Harry isn't around.'

Yvonne backed into an armchair. 'How dreadful. Poor Vivienne. What sort of a choice is that?'

'I know. Tragic, isn't it? But they're up there now in a rented house which goes with Harry's job.' Theo's worried look was replaced with a smile. 'And talking of work, you haven't started your job yet. What shall we do about it?'

'The school holidays start next week. I'm not sure how much time I can give to it. I could ask Ivy to have Susan, but I don't like to put upon her.' Yvonne was thinking of John's reaction to his mother looking after Susan while Yvonne spent more time with Theo, even if it was work.

'A person to set up displays would be useful, but what would be even more useful would be someone to do some cataloguing for me. I find it quite time-consuming and I'm not very patient or methodical. I can show you what's involved and it's something you could do at home. What do you say?'

Yvonne had the impression Theo might have manufactured the position just for her, but she liked the sound of it. 'I think I would enjoy that.' Although it wouldn't get her out of the house and mixing with new people, it would be a very welcome income.

'Good. Now's not the time to discuss it, though. I'm being distracted by delicious smells from the kitchen.'

Yvonne got up and served the melon. 'Would you like some wine with it?' she asked.

'Perhaps later. Ice-cold melon is just the right thing to serve on an evening like this. The heatwave seems to have been going on and on.' Just as he said it, there was a rumble of thunder and they started laughing. 'I've put a jinx on the weather now.'

*   ★   ★

'Is there any special reason for you to invite me over this evening?'

'I liked my time with you last weekend. What happened at the end of the evening out was unfortunate, but I thought it would be pleasant to spend some time with someone whose company I enjoyed. Did you mind me asking you? Do you think I'm forward?'

'A hussy in the making, I'd say,' said Theo.

'Then I've achieved what I set out to do,' giggled Yvonne. 'I just wanted to spread my wings a little, have some fun.'

'And are you? Having some fun? I am. I love being here with you. You're good company, an excellent cook, and you're amusing. We must do this more often, don't you think?'

'I think . . . I think I should serve up the pudding. Would you like another glass of wine? If so, please help yourself. I've had enough.' She hiccupped and Theo laughed.

The pudding came accompanied with a spark of lightning and a crash of thunder, and seconds later rain was lashing against the window panes. They watched in fascination the transformation of the sky to an inky black. Yvonne got up to draw over the curtains, but Theo said, 'Let's enjoy the performance, shall we? I like a magnificent thunderstorm.'

Later, over coffee and a couple of chocolates, they sat side by side on the rug, staring out at the rainy night. Yvonne was thinking how perfect the evening was when another sharp flash of lightning and a loud crash of thunder made her jump.

Theo had his arms around her in a moment. Then his lips bent to hers and they shared a kiss. Just as she thought he was pulling away from her, his embrace tightened and he lowered her gently to the floor. They lay facing each other as Theo traced a finger down her cheek and across her mouth. All Yvonne was aware of was a heartbeat — his or hers, she did not know — thudding quickly. She wanted him to kiss her, but didn't want to break away from the tender moment, so she stayed still. His breathing quickened and she knew it was up to her; would she let him go further or not? Theo made the decision by sitting up and saying, 'Gosh, that was some storm.'

'I should draw the curtains across.'

'Yes; who knows who might be passing and looking in your windows, Mrs Mitchell.'

At the mention of her title, Yvonne knew the time would come for her to tell Theo about Ted, but now was not it. 'Would you like more coffee?' she asked.

'I'd better be going. I've had the most wonderful evening. Perhaps next week I could take you and Susan for a drive somewhere. It's half-day closing on Wednesday and the schools are on holiday, so what do you say? We could go out to the river near Woodbridge, have a boat trip perhaps. And some fish and chips. Would you and Susan like that?'

'Yes, we would.' Yvonne felt excited, not just for herself, but for Susan, who would enjoy a day out.

Theo brushed Yvonne's cheek lightly with his lips and left.

★   ★   ★

Susan, although pleased to see her mum, didn't break off from the game she was playing with John. 'What a storm it was last night,' said Yvonne.

'Sunny again this morning, though. You could have had a lie-in, Yvonne,' said Ivy.

'I thought I could wheel you around to admire your neighbours' gardens. We haven't done that for ages.'

Ivy pushed the kitchen door half-shut. 'First of all, tell me about your evening. Is he good-looking, this man of yours?'

'He's not mine,' protested Yvonne.

'But you like him,' persisted Ivy.

At that moment, John came into the kitchen. 'I've come for a drink.' He poured two tumblers of orange squash and was about to return to the sitting room when he turned and blurted out, 'Why don't you ask Mr Theodore Egerton about his wife?'

29

Ivy had spoken sharply to John. She tried to excuse his words by whispering that her son was jealous. All Yvonne had on her mind was to get back to her own home. John had obviously asked Susan about Theo and found out his name, but where had he got information about a wife? Had he made it up or was there a basis for truth in what he'd said? Theo was definitely of an age to be married, and he was a handsome man. The flat didn't look as if a woman lived there. They might have separate homes. The possibilities were endless.

Susan was displeased at having been dragged away from her card game and was on the verge of a temper tantrum, something she rarely had. 'We must get home,' said Yvonne.

'I wanted to stay with John and Ivy,'

whined Susan. 'Why have we got to go home now?'

'Because I said so,' snapped Yvonne. She glanced at her daughter and softened. 'I'm sorry, Susan. I was upset. I know it's going to be hard for you to get used to being without Vivienne.'

Susan stopped suddenly. 'What's happened to Vivienne?'

Yvonne could have kicked herself. She'd forgotten Susan didn't know about Vivienne and her family moving. 'Vivienne is all right, Susan. They've moved house as her daddy's got a different job now. They've gone to live near the sea. Theo told me last night and I forgot you didn't know. Perhaps I can find out her address and you can write her a postcard.'

Susan cheered considerably.

Yvonne picked up and put down the telephone several times, wanting to get in touch with Theo yet dreading to hear what he would say. Her call was put through to The Lawns Hotel, where they transferred her to Theo's flat.

'Theo, it's Yvonne. I have to talk to you.'

'Sounds serious. What's the problem?'

'If I'm to come out with you on Wednesday, I must know something.' She took a deep breath. 'Have you got a wife?'

The silence from the other end of the telephone line stretched to infinity. Then a strained voice said, 'Why does having a wife make or break a drive to the river, Yvonne?'

Put like that, Yvonne had no answer. She'd thought Theo felt romantically about her, but from what he was saying, it didn't sound like it now. 'It doesn't, Theo. I'm sorry.' There was no reply as the call had been ended.

Now she had no future. No romance with someone she thought she was falling in love with. No job, as Theo certainly wouldn't want her on his staff now. And the secondary modern school was closed for the holiday, so she couldn't enquire there. And Susan was unhappy because her mother had spoilt her day. Feeling sorry for herself, Yvonne unhooked the locket and flung it across the room, where it hit the far wall and fell behind the sideboard. So much for it being an avenue back to happiness. All it had brought so far was misery. She sat in the chair until Susan came into the room sometime later.

'Why are you crying, Mummy?' She climbed onto her knee.

'I didn't know I was. Isn't that silly?' said Yvonne, sniffing, and hugging her daughter. 'I tell you what we could do. I was given some lovely chocolates last night by Theo. Do you think we should have a couple?'

'Ooh, yes please. And then are we going to have Sunday dinner?'

Yvonne had forgotten about a meal. 'As it's the start of the holidays tomorrow, shall we have a sandwich now and then eat our roast dinner this evening? You can stay up late as you don't have to go to school.' Susan's hugs and kisses told her she'd made the right decision.

*   *   *

The next morning, Susan was bright
and happy; Yvonne was not. She knew
she should speak to Theo again, but had
no idea what to say. When there was a
ring at the front door bell she assumed
it was the postman. But it was a serious-
looking Theo.

'Can I come in?'

Yvonne stood aside for him to enter
the hall. 'Go through to the dining
room.'

'Hello,' said Susan. 'Is Vivienne
happy to be living by the sea?'

'It will take her a while to get used
to being without her friends,' replied
Theo.

'Mummy said I could send her a
postcard,' said Susan.

'Then you'll need her address, won't
you?' He pulled out a notebook and pen
and handed over the address to Susan.
'I'm sure she'll be pleased to hear from
you.'

He then spoke to Yvonne. 'I've

brought over details of the cataloguing. I wondered if you might make a start this week.'

Yvonne was stunned. She hadn't expected that. Quickly, she said, 'I'm looking forward to it. Susan, what we're talking about will be very boring for you. Why don't you go and play?'

Susan skipped off and Yvonne tried to take in what Theo was saying. 'Could you manage to work ten hours a week? I know Susan will be around and she must be your priority. Your pay will be one pound and ten shillings a week. Now, if you're happy with that, I'll tell you what's required. You can show me how you're getting on when we meet on Wednesday. *If* we meet on Wednesday.' His face clouded over. 'You asked me about a wife.'

'I just wondered.' Yvonne was out of her depth and unsure how to answer. Damn John Palmer and his scandal-mongering.

'I *was* married,' said Theo, in a voice so low Yvonne had to move closer to hear his words. 'My wife died. She was run over on a zebra crossing. The doctors couldn't save her or our unborn child. I moved to Suffolk to be near Delia and her family. Ironic, as they've just moved away.'

Yvonne was horrified. What an appalling thing to have happened. 'I'm sorry, Theo.' She put her arms around him and stroked his back, just as she would have done to Susan if she were distressed. 'You don't deserve such a bad thing to happen to you.'

'How do you know?' There was a sad smile on his face.

'You're good with people. I saw your gentle side with Susan just now, and you were patient and kind to Vivienne and Delia.'

'Thank you. So are we going out on Wednesday?'

'Can I come?' Susan came into the room.

'Of course,' said Theo. 'You're the guest of honour.'

Susan bounded over to him and

hugged him. 'Could you be *my* Uncle Theo now that Vivienne has gone away?'

'Yes, I could, but I'll still be Vivienne's uncle as well.'

When Theo was leaving, Yvonne was alarmed to see John coming up the path. What did he want now?

'Can't you leave Yvonne alone? Haven't you done enough damage?' John swung back his arm and aimed a blow at Theo's jaw, which was skilfully foiled.

'I've no idea who you are or what you're talking about, but don't ever try to touch me again,' said Theo calmly. 'And have some respect for Yvonne and Susan, please.'

Yvonne shooed Susan indoors and said, 'John, apologise to Theo and then go away.'

John did as he was told, his face the colour of cooked beetroot, and then walked away down the path.

'He's a friend of mine,' explained Yvonne to Theo. 'Well, he was. I don't think he is anymore. He was the one who told me you were married. I think he's jealous, but he had no right to attack you.'

'No harm done,' murmured Theo. 'I'll be in touch.'

Yvonne had no idea how she was going to explain what had happened to Susan. She was very fond of both John and Theo. In the end, she decided to go and see Ivy. It was unlikely John would be there.

★   ★   ★

'Come in,' called Ivy when Yvonne knocked on her front door.

'Ivy, are you on your own? Can we talk in private?' whispered Yvonne.

'You play in here, Susan, and when I've had a chat to your mum, we can all do something together.'

The two women sat in the kitchen. 'John came round this morning,' said Yvonne. 'Theo was there. John would have knocked his block off if he hadn't defended himself well.'

Ivy took a sharp intake of breath. 'That's bad of him. I never thought I'd hear that sort of thing about my own son.' Ivy fished for a handkerchief from her cardigan sleeve and sobbed into it.

'I only told you so you might understand if I didn't come round much, unless I'm sure John isn't here. And I don't think it's a good idea for Susan to stay overnight with you either.'

Ivy nodded.

'Shall we all go for a walk around the houses and see the gardens? Let me get your wheelchair.'

Despite everything, Ivy looked at Yvonne cheekily and asked, 'What was this Theo doing at your house this morning?'

'He came to tell me about the job he's given me,' said Yvonne. 'I'll be earning money, Ivy. I can't wait.'

'Your life is taking a new direction. I wish you all you wish for yourself.'

Yvonne wanted happiness and good health for Susan; for herself, she wanted love and excitement. She wanted Theo Egerton. Perhaps the two of them might have a chance of romance after all.

30

Susan was thrilled when the day of the outing arrived, and the drive to Woodbridge was glorious. Sun had replaced the clouds of the previous day. With the top down, it was too noisy for much conversation in the car, but when they had to slow, they could hear Susan singing.

Theo appeared to know the area well, explaining that he sometimes came out to auction houses in the region. 'You could come with me if you like,' he invited Yvonne. 'You seem to have acquired a bit of interest in antiques, if I'm not mistaken.'

'What are antiques?' asked Susan.

Theo explained to Susan. Once again, Yvonne was impressed that Theo gave her such attention. By the time he'd finished explaining, they were walking beside the river and Theo was pointing out different birds and they were laughing at waddling and hissing swans.

Theo pointed to a notice. 'There's a short river trip due in quarter of an hour. Are you both good sailors?'

The day went by as planned, but the time came when they had to leave and head homewards. Susan was tired, but wanted to stay at Woodbridge for ever and ever, as she put it.

'If we go home now,' said Theo, 'we might have time to visit the park. Say goodnight to the fish in the goldfish pond. If that's all right with you, Yvonne?'

They reached the park, and as promised, Theo led Yvonne and Susan through the gateway. 'Ten minutes and then it will be time to go home,' said Yvonne.

Susan nodded and ran towards the pond, trailing her fingers in the murky water, trying to reach out to touch a lily pad. The grown-ups sat on a bench and Yvonne said, 'We've had a lovely day,

Theo, thank you. I wish you'd let me pay for something, though. I'm a working girl now.'

'If that's a hint you're wanting your pay, you'll have to wait until Friday.' He stood up and called, 'The ten minutes are up. Susan, come on, time to go.'

They looked around — no Susan. Where was she? Panic welled in Yvonne. This had never happened before; Susan was always very well behaved. 'Susan, come on, please don't hide from us.'

Theo was striding around the area, but Yvonne couldn't move. With every second that went by, icicles jabbed at her body. In a minute, she'd wake up and everything would be all right. But it wasn't all right. Susan didn't appear. Theo was shouting her name, but there was no response. Theo returned and stood over her. 'Stay here, Yvonne. If Susan comes back to the pond, she'll be worried if we're not here and might wander off again. I'll look over by the bandstand and the swings. Can you hear me, Yvonne? Stay here.'

Yvonne could hear Theo, and the alarm in his voice, which echoed her own fear. Where could Susan have gone? She had been only a few feet away from them while they were talking. The idyllic day would no longer be that, it would be the day Susan went missing. Where was she? Yvonne tried to call to her, but her voice refused to function. From a distance she heard voices and sensed movement, but could make no significance of it. Then Theo was at her side again.

'I've telephoned the police, Yvonne. They'll help us find Susan quickly.' He knelt beside her and held her hand. 'We're going home, in case Susan finds her way there.'

'You said she'd come here,' croaked Yvonne. 'I'm not moving.'

'The police are here now. I'll come with you. I'm not leaving you.' He tugged at her, but she wouldn't budge.

'You said to stay here,' she insisted. Her voice rose to a shout. 'Susan, Susan, where are you? You've found a good hiding place, but please come out now.' She looked around wildly, then back at Theo. 'Where is she?'

He ran his fingers through his hair. 'She'll be back soon. We're going home.'

This time she let him pull her up and lead her to his car, but she kept looking over her shoulder and screaming, 'Susan, please come out now.'

★   ★   ★

Theo helped Yvonne to a chair in the sitting room and put a pouffe under her feet. He went upstairs and got a blanket to put over her and made a pot of tea. Yvonne was shaking so hard, the hot liquid splashed over her hand, but she didn't flinch. She looked up at him. 'Where is she, Theo? When will she be home?'

A sharp knock on the front door was followed by a call of 'Police'. Theo opened the door and ushered the two men in.

'We're doing all we can to find your daughter. What would help us most at the moment is a photograph of her. Have you got one?'

'On the mantelpiece,' said Yvonne.

'You're the girl's father?' one of the men said to Theo.

'No, a friend of the family.'

'Where's her father?'

'I don't know,' replied Yvonne.

'What's his name?'

'Ted Lambert.'

'Does he live here?'

'No.'

'We'll need to trace him.' He gestured to his colleague, who wrote something in a notebook. 'Any reason your daughter, Susan isn't it, might run off? Did you have a quarrel? Is that what happened?'

Yvonne shook her head. Theo said, 'We'd had a nice day out and stopped off at the park for Susan to say goodnight to the goldfish before she came home to bed. Susan must have wandered off from the pond and couldn't find her way back. She's only six years old.'

The policeman nodded, but was busy writing things down. 'We'll be off. Please stay in the house and let us know if Susan turns up.' The two men left.

'She will, won't she?'

'The police will be able to scour the park. She'll be found.'

In the early hours of the morning, Yvonne's eyes closed and she sank in the void of sleep. A short while later, she was awake again and reality took its hold. She searched the house. 'She's not here. Where is she? Is this my punishment for thinking I would be happy? If so, I'll exchange anything I have for my darling Susan to come home.'

'I know,' crooned Theo, who had followed her around like a shadow. He took her in his arms and cradled her head against his chest. 'Dear Yvonne, I hate to see you like this. I'm here, my dearest. I'll stay with you.'

Yvonne leant against him, heard his murmurs, but couldn't make out the words. It didn't matter. Nothing mattered except Susan coming home. Theo lowered her onto the bed and covered her with a bedspread. 'Rest if you can.'

Yvonne had never experienced such bleakness. Susan had to come home soon. What could have happened to her? She didn't want to think about it, yet images of her child lying injured somewhere floated into her mind, only to be replaced with equally graphic ones of someone taking her — and harming her.

Theo sat next to her, holding her hand until the birds woke up.

'Susan will be very frightened,' whispered Yvonne. 'I want her here with me. Please, Theo, I must have her here.'

A commotion outside made both of them get up and go to the front window. A policeman was talking to someone on the pavement. A man walked up the front path with a bundle in his arms. Yvonne gasped and threw open the front door. 'Susan, oh Susan, you're safe now, darling. Come here.' She grabbed the child and clasped her tightly, but she was sleeping.

'John?' said Theo, looking at the man who had brought Susan home. 'What have you been up to?'

31

The policeman came to the house. 'I've telephoned the station. My superior will be here shortly.'

A few minutes later, a knock at the door heralded the arrival of the senior policeman. 'This is Susan? Your daughter, Mrs Mitchell?'

'Oh yes, this is definitely Susan. Please speak quietly, she's asleep.'

'We'll need to know if she's been hurt,' said the policeman. 'A doctor's on his way.' He turned to John. 'And who are you?'

'John Palmer. A friend of the family.'

'We'll need to interview you, Mr Palmer. The police car outside will take you to the station. Come along please, sir.' He hurried John out of the house.

The doctor pronounced Susan well and unharmed, apart from having spent a night out of doors, and she wouldn't have to go to the hospital. Yvonne carried her daughter upstairs, and the two of them got into Yvonne's bed fully clothed and cuddled up together.

'I'm glad to be home, Mummy. I had a lovely time today.' She turned into her mother's arms and fell asleep again.

Yvonne didn't sleep; she spent the next few hours enjoying the warmth of her child and the relief of having her home safe and well.

★　★　★

'John, you're a hero. Thank you for finding Susan.' Yvonne gave him a kiss on the cheek. 'How did you know where to find her?'

'I didn't know. When I heard she was missing, I had to go and help look for her. I thought as the police were in the park they would find her if she was there. Then I remembered that house outside the gates of the park has a child's playhouse she used to dawdle around sometimes when we took her out. If only I'd thought of it sooner.'

'I won't ever be able to repay you for what you did, John. Thank you.'

He smiled at her, shook Theo's hand and went off to work.

'I must get to work as well,' said Theo. 'You'll be all right on your own?'

'I'm not on my own. I've got Susan here — where she belongs.'

Yvonne was curious as to why Susan had left the park. The police would want to know as well, but she wasn't going to ask questions about it now.

They sat down with large slices of sponge cake accompanied by milk for Susan and coffee for Yvonne. She'd had enough cups of tea over the previous hours to last her a lifetime.

'Can we have a dog, Mummy?'

'We'll see,' replied Yvonne, automatically.

'That means no.' Susan had another mouthful of cake and tried again. 'I'd really like to have a dog. I wonder if Vivienne has one.'

'Let's see how my new job goes first.

I might have to go into Theo's shop sometimes to work and it's not fair to leave a dog on its own for long.'

'Can we have one like the dog in the park?'

Yvonne was immediately alert. Trying to sound off-hand, she asked, 'What dog was that?'

'The one I followed. I think he was lost. Then he ran off and *I* was lost.'

'Is that when you went into the little house and fell asleep?' asked Yvonne.

Susan nodded. 'What are we doing today?'

'Shall we telephone Ivy?'

Ivy was pleased to speak to Susan, and Yvonne asked her to thank John again and said that they'd be round to visit her soon.

'Would you like to go shopping, Susan? Or are you feeling tired after yesterday?'

'I'm not tired.'

'I thought we might see if there's a bicycle for you in the town.'

Susan threw herself at her mother.

'I'd like a bicycle. Will I be able to ride it? Are my legs long enough?'

'You can try some out in the shop. I'd like to buy you a present which you can enjoy during the holidays.'

The bicycle shop had just the thing for Susan, a sturdy red bike which she would need a bit of practice with, but by the look on her face she'd be willing to ride it every hour she was allowed. The shop promised to deliver it the following morning.

Despite her earlier protestations, as soon as they returned home, Susan curled up on the rug on the sitting room floor and was fast asleep within minutes. Yvonne sat watching her and was grateful her daughter had been returned to her.

★ ★ ★

'Hello, what's that you've got there?' asked Theo when he called round to see Susan and Yvonne the following day.

'My new bicycle,' said Susan with a

353

smile. 'It's the same colour as your car. I think I can go faster than you.' She wobbled off around the garden, which was really too small for bicycle riding.

'Susan's all right, is she?'

'Yes, she seems to be. Have you come with more work?'

'You make me sound like a slave driver. As a matter of fact, I've given up my meal break to bring you your wages.' He handed over a small brown envelope.

'Thank you. Will you have a cup of tea? Or something to eat?'

'I'd love to stay, but I have to get back. My assistant — my *other* assistant — is expecting me. I've got a bit of news, though. Harry got in touch with me and asked if I would like to visit him and Vivienne in Cromer. He also wondered if you and Susan would like to go as well.'

'That sounds just the thing for the school holidays. A trip to see a friend. Susan will love it and I shall, too.'

'Good. I'll let him know. I'll drive

you up there a week tomorrow after I've shut the shop. We'll stay the night and come back after tea on Sunday. Does that sound all right?' Yvonne nodded.

Theo made a point of saying cheerio to Susan, who was busy puffing round and round the garden trying not to fall off her bicycle too many times.

★   ★   ★

At last they were on their way to Cromer. Both Yvonne and Susan had been excited to pack a case for their overnight stay and Susan had been hopping around, waiting for Theo to arrive.

According to Theo, they'd made good time and were soon approaching the town. 'You can see the sea if you peep between those houses.'

Harry and Vivienne opened the front door before they'd had time to knock. The house was enormous. Yvonne felt a pang of jealousy. Then she reminded herself of the difficulties of the family who lived there. She wouldn't want that for anything. Vivienne gave Susan a big hug and took her away to play.

'They'll be all right,' said Harry. 'Yvonne, I was sorry to hear Susan went missing, but I'm pleased she was found safe and sound.'

'It was a relief. How's Delia? Is she any better?'

'She's happy enough at the centre. Lives in. Doesn't come home or express a desire to do so. I can't tell if the treatment's working, but it's the only help available.' He looked miserable.

'We've come to cheer you up,' said Theo, bringing in the cases. 'Where shall I put these?'

'I thought the two girls could share a room. A bit of an adventure for them. Follow me, I'll show you both around.'

The girls were in Vivienne's bedroom playing with a toy kitchen set. 'Vivienne's got lots of toys. She says I can sleep in her room. Look, she's got *two* beds here.' The chatter continued and the grown-ups moved on.

Harry was an attentive host, and while the children had an early meal, he told them all about the pier and the shows he and Vivienne had seen there. 'I'll take you to the beach tomorrow,' he said. 'There's a Punch and Judy show and we'll be able to have a paddle.'

'We'll look forward to that,' said Yvonne. She was curious. 'Harry, how do you manage in the house and go out to work? You must be a miracle man.'

'I wish I was. I have a resident housekeeper to do the miracles. She has Saturday afternoon and evenings off, but she's prepared our meal and it's sitting in a hostess trolley. She's also around to look after Vivienne when I'm working.'

'Would she like to come and work for me?' laughed Theo.

'Not a chance,' replied Harry.

'Shall I take the girls up then? Get them ready for bed and let you two men have a chat together.'

'Sure you don't mind? If would be a very big help.'

When Yvonne returned, they sat at the dining table and Harry wheeled in the trolley. The starter of consommé soup was delicious, not too filling, so there was plenty of room for the aromatic boeuf bourguignon and accompanying sliced potatoes in a creamy sauce.

'This is excellent,' said Theo, tucking in heartily.

'Adèle is French,' explained Harry between mouthfuls. 'She'll be pleased you like her cooking.'

The pudding of Charlotte Russe completed the best meal Yvonne had ever eaten and she told Harry.

'You'll have to tell Adèle when you see her in the morning.'

Yvonne volunteered to wheel the trolley full of empty dishes and dirty crockery and cutlery into the kitchen. Coffee was definitely needed, so she put the kettle on and hunted out cups and saucers. There were a couple of devices she recognised as a cafetière and a percolator, but she had never used them before, so was pleased to spot a tin of instant coffee.

'That's good of you, Yvonne. Thank you. There you are, Theo — Yvonne is as much a miracle worker as Adèle, so why not get her to come and work for you?'

'She already does,' laughed Theo.

Yvonne could stifle her yawns no longer. 'I'm going up. See you tomorrow.'

'I hope it's all right, but Harry has said I can visit Delia at the centre in the morning. Apparently mornings are better than afternoons for her, and I'd like to see her. We'll go to the beach when we get back.'

'Of course. I'm glad you'll be able to see your sister. I'm sure we can amuse ourselves here.'

★　★　★

The girls were up and out of their room when Yvonne went in to wake them. She found them in the dining room.

'Hello, Mummy. We've been up for

ages. Adèle helped us get ready. She's cooking breakfast.'

The door swung open, and a very fashionable curvy lady of about thirty-five came through with dishes of eggs, bacon, tomatoes and fried potatoes, which she put on the table, instructing them all to help themselves. 'So you are Yvonne. How do you do? I am Adèle.'

Yvonne took in the stylish clothes. Adèle's hair was wrapped into an elaborate chignon and her fingernails were painted vermilion. Not the usual sort of housekeeper, Yvonne thought. When Harry and Theo came in to say goodbye, she noticed the look between Harry and Adèle and wondered if they were having an affair.

'I must say thank you for our delicious food last night, and breakfast looks like another tasty meal. I wish I had your talents,' Yvonne said.

'I enjoy cooking. Harry is most appreciative of my efforts.' She winked at Yvonne, who was left speechless. It seemed that not only was Adèle having an affair, she was flaunting the fact.

Yvonne helped herself to a piece of toast and then said, 'Have you known Harry long?'

'Yes. If he hadn't asked me to look after him and Vivienne, I would have volunteered. It's a lovely house to live in and I enjoy the job. There are also perks.' She held out her hands to show off a display of rings and turned her head from side to side so Yvonne could see her earrings, which looked like diamonds. 'You're on your own, aren't you? I mean without a husband. I could introduce you to someone if you like. Wouldn't you like a few perks?'

Shocked, with herself as much as what Adèle had proposed, Yvonne wondered if she would.

32

Back at home after a whirlwind of a weekend by the sea, Yvonne laughed to herself as she remembered Adèle's suggestion. Of course she'd dismissed the idea, but couldn't deny it had been in her head. As soon as Theo had come into the room, she'd known she only wanted to be with him.

After Susan was in bed, Theo accepted Yvonne's invitation to stay for coffee and he told her about Delia.

'I can't understand why she turned to alcohol,' he admitted. 'She had everything she wanted in Harry and Vivienne. I will go and see her again soon.'

Yvonne wondered if Delia knew about Harry and Adèle. Perhaps there had been other women before her and that was why she sought an escape. Her dream had slipped through her fingers. Yvonne didn't want secrets kept from Theo; she had to tell him about her past. 'Theo, I think you deserve to know things regarding Susan's father. When she was missing, I told the police about him, and it's unfair for you to know half the story.' Yvonne told him what she'd told Delia and waited for his reaction.

'All I can say is that you're making a fine job of bringing up Susan on your own. Your personal background makes no difference to me.' He pulled her out of the chair and put his arms around her, his lips meeting hers. Yvonne found the comfort she needed in his tender embrace and hoped he found it too from hers. They stayed entwined for some time, as if neither wanted to let the other go.

* * *

Later in the week, Yvonne sat in the sitting room. Idly, she reached for her locket. It wasn't there. Of course, she'd flung it across the room. Where had it ended up?

Behind the sideboard. This particular piece of furniture proved a challenge she couldn't manage. It would not yield. One big push was needed and she screamed as the heavy object fell.

Yvonne groaned as she lay on the floor. Her face was wet and she wondered why. A sharp pain split across her eyes and she felt sick. It was nearly time to collect Susan, so she had to get up. The room twisted around and she felt dizzy. It was a bit more comfortable to keep her eyes shut. Five minutes was all she needed, then she'd get Susan.

'Yvonne, it's all right, I'm here. Can you open your eyes? Wake up if you can.' Yvonne didn't want to rouse herself from the wonderful dream she was having. Theo was with her, his hand on her head, his voice soothing her. 'Can you hear me, darling?'

'Yes, my love, I hear you,' she replied.

'Please open your eyes,' said Theo.

Briefly, Yvonne fluttered open her eyelids. It really was Theo. She wasn't asleep and dreaming, but awake and

. . . on the floor. 'Help me up. I have to get to Susan.'

'Thank goodness you're responding, but please lie still. You've had an accident. Susan is safe. I brought her home from school.'

Hearing what he said, Yvonne lay back and closed her eyes. 'The locket. The sideboard fell over.'

'You've hurt your head, and I've telephoned the doctor, who will be here soon. I'll go and tell Susan you're awake and then I'll be back with you. If I had my way, I'd never leave you.'

★　★　★

The doctor said Yvonne should go to the hospital for stitches to her head and to be checked for concussion.

Once back home again, Theo stayed with her and took Susan to school the following morning. He was soon back and by her side. 'What can I get for you?' he asked.

Yvonne smiled and held out her

hand, not at all embarrassed she was in her nightdress and in bed. 'I'd like a cuddle, please.'

Theo snuggled up to her on the bed, and this time it was Yvonne who initiated the kiss. 'You found it then,' she said, when at last they broke apart.

'What? What did I find?'

'The locket.'

Theo fished in his pocket and brought it out. 'Yes. It was behind the sideboard. I wonder how it got there.'

'It's a long story,' said Yvonne, reaching for it.

'How did you know I'd got it?'

'Because happiness is returning.' Theo fixed the locket around Yvonne's neck and she touched it lightly. 'Why did you meet Susan from school yesterday?'

'They were worried when there was no one to meet her. They telephoned me and you know the rest.'

'Thank you, Theo. But you mustn't stay here with me, much as I'm enjoying your company. You've a business to run.'

'I'm taking some time off. I'm staying with you and Susan. If that's all right.'

'Theo, I think I'm falling in love with you.'

'And I know I'm in love with you, Yvonne. I've known it almost from the first moment I saw you, but I didn't want to plunge into something where I might end up hurting you, or — I must be honest — getting hurt myself.'

Yvonne remembered his wife and unborn child, and tears blurred her vision. She reached for him and they clung to each other.

★　★　★

Love comes in so many ways, thought Yvonne later that night as she and Theo wrapped themselves around each other. She touched the locket.

'I love you, my darling,' she said, raising her face to his to receive another kiss.

'And I love you. I always will.'

33

RACHEL — *Present day*

Rachel had come prepared with several large bags. It had been a very successful morning at the car boot sale. The early spring sunshine warmed her face. What a great way to spend Sunday morning, taking their time, browsing the stalls, snacking on bacon rolls and hot coffee.

'Happy?' asked Roy, strolling along beside her.

'As always,' she replied. 'Can I just have a look over there? I won't be long.'

'We've all the time in the world,' he replied. 'Let me take the bags, I'll catch you up.'

Rachel felt the thrill of making a mysterious discovery. Under the stall she headed for was a box full of unknown articles. She was itching to root through it.

'How much for this box?' she asked.

'Twenty pounds the lot,' was the reply.

Rachel still loved to haggle. 'Ten?'

The woman shook her head. 'I couldn't go that low. How about fifteen?'

It was a bargain. 'Yeah, okay. Thanks.'

Rachel handed over the money just as Roy arrived. 'I'm ready to go now,' she told him, 'unless you want to look at anything special.'

'I am.' He beamed down at her. 'Some*one* very special.'

Together they wandered towards the car, mulling over the possibilities for the day ahead.

Mo was away again. She'd been on several activity weekends, city breaks and holidays abroad, and now she was spending a few days with the U3A walking group in Northumberland. She hoped to visit Renata in Spain soon too.

Rachel and Roy had been busy, of course. First on the agenda had been getting to know each other properly, peeling off their layers and realising they adored what lay within. Roy had been amazingly helpful in a practical and loving way without being domineering and had helped her move her belongings to Mo's house, as well as assisting with the legal side of the rental of her flat. What Rachel had feared could be a major upheaval was dealt with as simply as a smile.

Rachel knew that Roy had her best interests at heart and now understood why he'd sounded rather stern when he'd said there was more to life than the daily grind. His father had put too much of himself into his work, to the detriment of his family and health.

Rachel fingered her locket. It still contained the images of the people she felt she'd got to know through Roy's musings about them. He'd given them names and invented stories surrounding them. The locket was more than a lucky charm, it was part of her.

'What time are you meeting the others?' asked Roy, transferring the contents of the bags to the kitchen table when they arrived back at Mo's house.

'Half one.'

Roy said, 'You'll have to leave soon. Will we meet tomorrow?'

'I'll give you a ring around half six.'

'Perfect. Have a good time this afternoon.'

★   ★   ★

The others were waiting for her and they shared a group hug, giggling at themselves.

'You don't know what it means to have you guys around again,' said Rachel. 'I got so involved in the café I neglected my best friends. Thank you for not giving up on me.'

Liz and Claire already had tissues to their eyes; Gillian, as usual, was a bit more subdued. 'It wasn't just the café, Rachel. We know your relationship with Michael was a bit challenging sometimes. Now you seem very happy with Roy. He's a lovely man. Anyway, we're all pleased to be a gang again, aren't we?'

The others nodded, and the four of them set off to a nearby hotel for some food and a chat.

The afternoon with her friends had been wonderful. Rachel was delighted they were welded together again.

⋆　⋆　⋆

When her phone rang, she answered it without looking to see who the caller was.

'Rachel, it's your father,' her mother's voice said.

'What's he done now, Mum?' Panic rose in Rachel. 'He's not ill, is he?'

'Ill? He's never ill. No, he's got a new venture. He asked me to tell you about it. So, are you sitting comfortably?'

When her mother finally stopped explaining, Rachel opened her mouth, but no words came out. Eventually, she managed, 'No, he can't do that.'

Her mother snorted down the phone.

'He's not very good at taking no for an answer, you should know that.'

'Can I think about it?'

'He had a feeling you'd say that.'

★ ★ ★

Rachel was surprised how quickly she was getting through her list of things to sort out. The next evening she rang Roy and told him to come to Mo's house.

'Good day?' she asked him when he arrived.

'Not bad, and yours? Are you going to bring me up to date with all the gossip from your friends?'

'They're a great bunch. I love them all and, yes, there is news.' Rachel waited until he was settled in the kitchen with a glass of wine. 'I had a call from Mum. You know what Dad's like with his new ventures?' Roy grinned and nodded. 'Well, the latest scheme is that he comes in with me on the restaurant. On paper only, he said, which means he doesn't get a share of

373

the profits or the money side particularly, just an input into the running of it.'

'How would that work, exactly?'

'He wants to devise ways of running a profitable business, by trying his ideas out on me.'

'And you're happy with that?'

'After some thought, yes, I am.'

'Fantastic. A good decision on your part then, as usual.'

'Also, he's insistent that he gives me a sizeable cheque for letting him try his ideas out.' Rachel smiled. 'I think it's just a ruse to get me to take his money, but it could be a mutually beneficial arrangement.'

'I'll help in any way I can, but this is your venture and I have every confidence you will make a success of it,' said Roy.

34

Rachel was still living in Mo's house, and her aunt had returned from yet another trip away. They were having a cosy night in together chatting about Mo's still-hectic lifestyle, Rachel's restaurant, her parents and finally, Roy.

'He's the one, is he?' asked Mo.

Rachel nodded. 'Definitely.'

'So you'll be moving in with him somewhere, will you?' asked Mo.

'Nothing's been said.'

'You'll have to ask him, then, and let me know what he says. I need to know if I can let your room,' said Mo, taking a swig of wine.

'Are you evicting me, Auntie Monica?'

'I just want to hurry your happiness along a bit, that's all. You know what I'm like, Rachel. Although the rent would come in handy . . . ' Then she held up her hands and laughed. 'Of course, I'm joking. I love you being here. You've brought joy to my life ever since you were a tiny child.'

★   ★   ★

The conversation stayed with Rachel until she next met up with Roy. The idea of living with him in a place of their own was tempting and exciting.

'Roy, how do you see us moving forward?' She cringed at the stupid wording she'd chosen.

'Aren't we all right as we are?' He seemed puzzled. Then his eyebrows shot up, his eyes twinkled and he blurted out, 'Rachel, I have something I'd like to say. You know I love you. Would you marry me, please?' He held out a lovers' knot ring and looked into her eyes with such tenderness that Rachel could feel tears forming. Everything was a blur, except her love for Roy.

Inelegantly, she sniffed. 'We belong together, Roy. I love you. I'd be honoured to be your wife.'

Later, she'd add a memento to the locket to represent another story in its life. The past was past, but a tantalising future lay ahead.

We do hope that you have enjoyed reading this large print book.

Did you know that all of our titles are available for purchase?

We publish a wide range of high quality large print books including:
Romances, Mysteries, Classics
General Fiction
Non Fiction and Westerns

Special interest titles available in large print are:
The Little Oxford Dictionary
Music Book, Song Book
Hymn Book, Service Book

Also available from us courtesy of Oxford University Press:
Young Readers' Dictionary
(large print edition)
Young Readers' Thesaurus
(large print edition)

For further information or a free brochure, please contact us at:
Ulverscroft Large Print Books Ltd.,
The Green, Bradgate Road, Anstey,
Leicester, LE7 7FU, England.
Tel: (00 44) 0116 236 4325
Fax: (00 44) 0116 234 0205